BLUESCHILD BABY

BLUESCHILD BABY

A NOVEL

GEORGE CAIN

ecco

An Imprint of HarperCollins*Publishers*

BLUESCHILD BABY. Copyright © 1970, 1994, 2019 by George Cain. Foreword copyright © 1994 by Gerald Early. Introduction © 2019 by Leslie Jamison. All rights reserved. Printed in the United States of America. No part of this book may be used or reproduced in any manner whatsoever without written permission except in the case of brief quotations embodied in critical articles and reviews. For information, address HarperCollins Publishers, 195 Broadway, New York, NY 10007.

HarperCollins books may be purchased for educational, business, or sales promotional use. For information, please email the Special Markets Department at SPsales@harpercollins.com.

Parts of the Introduction appeared in *The New Yorker* piece *Why George Cain's Blueschild Baby should be in the Addiction Canon* (March 2018), which was excerpted from Leslie Jamison's book *The Recovering* (Little, Brown and Company, 2018.)

Originally published in 1987 by Ecco Press.

FIRST ECCO PAPERBACK EDITION PUBLISHED 2019.

The Ecco Press and the author would like to acknowledge Jeanne Wilmot Carter for helping to bring this book back into print.

Designed by Michelle Crowe

Library of Congress Cataloging-in-Publication Data has been applied for.

ISBN 978-0-06-291316-6

19 20 21 22 23 LSC 10 9 8 7 6 5 4 3 2 1

For all those who loved and helped me:
My mother, father, family and friends.
Jo Lynne and Nataya

AL-HAMDU-LI-LA

FOREWORD

"... A FUGITIVE AND A VAGABOND shalt thou be in the earth." And so God pronounced the curse on Cain, murderer of his brother Abel in the book of Genesis, condemned to be an outsider, an alien, a wanderer, a marked, marginal man. Harlem-born and bred George Cain, protagonist of *Blueschild Baby,* like his biblical namesake exists in the pages of this frankly autobiographical novel as a marginal man, a vagabond, a fugitive, a wanderer, marked literally and figuratively by his drug addiction. He exists in a predatory world of junkies and hustlers whose code (in a Hobbesian world of capitalism and self-interest run riot) is the destruction of their brothers if it will stave off their own or bring them some profit. On one level, this novel is poised to answer the question: Am I indeed my brother's keeper? Here is a novel that gives us the amoral picaro as redeemed prodigal son. As George Cain, the narrator, writes: "The only place we see our oppression or what we have become is in the faces and actions of our brothers."

Blueschild Baby opens and closes, appropriately, with scenes involving commerce and consumption. In the opening, George Cain buys heroin from Flower and Sun (Sunflower?). In the end, his redemptive act of consumption, in the company of Nandy, the black woman who saves him, is the purchase of a necklace with a monkey's head from an outdoor stand selling African jewelry. The monkey, of course, signifies not only the drug habit Cain has successfully kicked, but the African and spiritual heritage he can rightfully reclaim now that he is no longer owned by the "white goddess" of heroin or the white women of the white world that once seduced him. His last purchase would suggest his transformation from Cain to Cane—alluding to the title of the classic 1923 work by Jean Toomer—a movement from alienation to immersion, from trying to find himself in the white world to rooting himself within the black community both locally and internationally. But in the journey that Cain takes, the reader must be careful not to see the novel exclusively as an unambiguous yearning for community and immersion. The novel pushes and pulls toward and against a set of complex, contrasting impulses.

Blueschild Baby, first published in 1970, is a bildungsroman, an education novel in much the same mode as *The Autobiography of Malcolm X, The Education of Sonny Carson,* Claude Brown's *Manchild in the Promised Land,* Eldridge Cleaver's *Soul on Ice,* Etheridge Knight's *Black Voices from Prison,* and George Jackson's *Soledad Brothers.* In other words, it is a product of mid-to-late 1960s and early 1970s black male confessional writing, usually combining two or more elements of the "black experience" as popularly understood at that time: the black criminal underground or the black underclass, with graphic details of prison, street hustling, drug addiction, and various moral and perverted sexual adventures with a variety of white and black women. It was the era when the novels of Iceberg Slim, a former street hustler, were must-reads and when Melvin Van Peebles's independent film, *Sweet Sweetback's Baadasssss Song,* about a black male sex performer on the lam, was probably the most noteworthy and most politically self-conscious of the so-called blaxploitation films and the only X-rated film that brought out the black community in droves to support it. Urban race riots (or rebellions, as some called them) were a commonplace in major cities in the summer; the Black Power Movement, in some significant measure, a kind of militant black youth movement, was in full sway; the F.B.I. had declared war on black militant groups such as the Black Panthers and some members of these groups responded in both a baiting and irresponsible manner by publicly advocating the murder of white police officers. Gil Scott-Heron and the Last Poets chanted poetry about the coming of the revolution; while James Brown, sporting an afro after years of wearing a process, sang about being black and proud.

It must be remembered, too, that the 1960s popularized illegal drug-taking as both an expression of charismatic youth and as a revolt against the establishment. Rock stars, literary figures, leading intellectual figures, dissidents, and many young people from all walks of life in the United States all openly discussed and even, in instances, advocated the virtue of taking drugs. This license-cum-political-and-therapeutic expression naturally had an effect, mostly destructive, on the national black urban community where a drug scourge in the late 1950s had previously wreaked havoc.

Much of the era's romantic obsession with the underclassed black male as political revolutionary stems first from the 1965 martyrdom of Malcolm X, the ex-hustler-turned-Muslim/Pan Africanist-firebrand and second, from the youthful, bourgeois view of the black criminal and underclass as inherently revolutionary (mainly because their often pathological behavior was seen as a form of resistance to white power and authority in much the same way as imprisoned opposition political leaders in Third World countries battling western colonialism). Serving time in prison gained such charismatic magnitude among young blacks, both the working classes and the bourgeoisie, in the late 1960s and early 1970s that at times the general attitude seemed little different than that of teenaged gang boys bragging to each other about doing time for "coppin' a homicide." "'Say it to yourself,'" J.B., one of the characters in *Blueschild Baby,* says to the corner boys, "'Yes, I'm a criminal and I'm free.'" Or as Cain's narrator puts it:

> The revolution shall begin in the penitentiaries and spread over the country for this is where the most aware minds are. They say you're arrested for crime, narcotics, prostitution, robbery, murder, but these are not the reasons for locking you away. Awareness is your crime, for once you become aware, you cannot help reacting in a manner contrary to the system that oppresses you. Very few commit crime because they enjoy doing so. They do what they have to. So many leaders are convicts. Awareness is a crime and sanity the only insanity, they are such rare qualities these days, they go unrecognized for what they are and are seen only as deviate from the madness that is normalcy.

Yet this view is challenged by novel's end when Cain is told by a street-corner character: ". . . hustling . . . ain't nothing but degradation." Further, the character Stacy informs Cain that his pursuit of worldly success and legitimation is so that the community itself can have hope and a future. Criminality, Cain learns, will neither free him nor give him solidarity.

From the standpoint of literary history, the aesthetic and even political origin of much of this cycle of African American literature is, on the one hand, rooted in the work of Jean Genet, Nelson Algren, William Burroughs, and Henry Miller. On the other hand, the violent, absurdist realism of Chester Himes and Rich-ard Wright are obvious and important models as well. In other words, George Cain came to his work with a well-defined and well-developed set of traditions from which to borrow and cre-ated a black anti-bourgeois novel that seizes and exploits a stan-dard bourgeois convention: namely, that the protagonist, with the love and help of a good woman, finds himself in this world and resurrects himself from his own filth.

George Cain began his autobiographical novel at the age of twenty-three in 1966 and finished it at age twenty-seven. It shows the occasional flaws of both a first novel and a novel by a young writer. Nonetheless, it has power and a surprising level of com-plexity. A number of worlds are evoked as a variety of circles that surround and constrict Cain's life, interpenetrating yet remain-ing distinct and discrete modes of existence and, more important, systems of values. There is Harlem, from the junky flophouses to the projects, then, Greenwich Village where Cain lives with his Italian American girlfriend, the world of upper-middle-class Brey Academy and the rich but outcast Jew, lower-middle-class urban New Jersey, the snobbish, superficial society of the professional black middle class, and the bureaucratic atmosphere of the parole office. But there is the even deeper density of the main character himself, split as he is between author/narrator and protagonist, between fiction and fact, and finally between what blacks and whites see him as and what he wishes to be himself. For despite the militancy and his urge for community, George Cain's quest and redemption are ultimately for himself. Although Nandy represents solidarity, roots, and the community, he does not, in the end, fully embrace that community; for his liberation from drugs is a liberation from having to prove himself to his com-munity, to become its hero and the one who made it. The drugs are a way for him to repudiate that burden—but throwing off the drugs is not Cain's resumption of the role of symbolic race uplifter, symbolic class jumper and race model. As Cain states in the beginning:

> It's like the other niggers in the joint who called me brother, automatically assuming because I was black, having shared the experience of blackness, we were closer than say two other people meeting for the first time. But it ain't so, a black is as treacherous as a white, all bear watching and familiarity does breed contempt.

And at novel's end:

> Everyone else seemed obliged only to themselves, while I was striving for Brey Prep that had given me a scholarship, my mother, father, brothers, people, for the sacrifices and faith they'd placed in me. Everyone but me had a piece of George Cain. Was no longer me, but a composite of all their needs and desires.

Unlike Bigger Thomas in *Native Son,* George Cain does not find and free himself in the utter paradox, the complete contradiction, of becoming, embracing precisely the thing, the being that society made him. *Blueschild Baby* offers another vision, a different philosophical possibility, that George Cain can free himself only by insisting with all his strength that he must not be what either whites or blacks insist: race hero, junkie, basketball star, sex-crazed "darkie." And it is in this that the Islamic trappings of the novel become important. The term "Al-Hamdu-Li-La" used in the dedication means something like "all praises due to Allah," and Cain's brother's conversion to Islam indicates less an attraction to Islam specifically as a complex historical theology than a mood of purification from the vile corruption of western whites and their view of the world.

Blueschild Baby's return to print means it can now be read in proper context with the other two major novels of its day: John A. Williams's *The Man Who Cried I Am* and James Baldwin's *Tell Me How Long the Train's Been Gone,* forming a literary triad as striking and as rich in defining its time as any in African American literary history. Moreover, it can be seen not only as a product of its time but as both an aesthetic encapsulation and fulfillment of its remarkable vision.

GERALD EARLY
ST. LOUIS, MISSOURI, 1993

INTRODUCTION

B LUESCHILD BABY TAKES PLACE during the summer of 1967—the summer of race riots all across the nation; the Summer of Love in the Haight-Ashbury; the summer of marines dying near Con Thien, across the world in Vietnam—but the novel illuminates the contours of a more private hell: the angry desperation of a young heroin addict. Its world is an orchestra of noise and need and possibility, traveling the streets of Manhattan from Harlem to the West Village: housing projects buzzing with hawkers and ice cream truck bells; window curtains flapping in the humidity; Sam Cooke lilting from a kitchen radio: *It's been too hard living / but I'm afraid to die*; and a drunk swaying to the rhythms of his voice in the streets below. It's a world full of summer heat radiating from asphalt and sun-softened tar; neon signs glinting off cars outside nightclubs deep into the night, and fruit vendors hosing down sidewalks at dawn; a love song to the city, a dirge for its lost souls, and an ode to their struggle.

More than anything, *Blueschild Baby* is a picaresque of scoring and trying to stop. The novel follows a young black man—named George Cain, like his author—after his release from prison. Its plot is the primal and well-trodden arc of every addiction story: He is not supposed to use. He keeps using. Eventually, he tries to quit for good. The novel is an unvarnished conjuring of the tyranny of dependence: its desperation, its degradation, its rage and rebellion; the fragile, unsettled, occasional shards of hope it permits; the strange, searing joys of being alive and young and lost and hooked and full of feverish determination anyway.

When *Blueschild Baby* was published, the *New York Times* called it "the most important work of fiction by an Afro-American since 'Native Son,'" but Cain has fallen into utter obscurity since then. When he died of complications from liver disease in 2010— just shy of his sixty-seventh birthday, forty years after that glowing review—the *Times* ran an obituary that described Cain as a promising voice whose potential was never realized: "Drugs dashed these hopes."

Blueschild Baby reads like a book-length attempt to exorcise with fiction what Cain couldn't purge from his body. Cain understood the ravages of heroin as well as anyone, and his novel summons that devastation without mercy or reserve: a pusher shoving ice up a woman's vagina to bring her back from an overdose, or a "haunted huddle" of junkies "nodding, stinking, burning, high," lit by the glow of a TV playing cartoons. When George visits the projects where he was born, he gets a junkie named Fix to cop for him, "gaunt and hollow . . . skin strapped tight around the skull . . . there's not enough junk in the world to quench his need." When he visits "Sun the Pusher" in his apartment off Amsterdam Avenue, he describes the smell—a combination of sulphur, cigarettes, and decaying flesh—as reminiscent of the rotten "yellow mist" rising from dead crickets in the courtyard of a Texas penitentiary, where George had been serving time on drug charges.

This novel is deeply alive to the physical and emotional horrors of addiction, but it also understands that criminalizing addicts only compounds this damage. It is a difficult, prickly book in part because it's trying to tell two stories that sit together uneasily: the damage of drugs, and the ways this damage has been deployed as moralizing rhetoric.

In her book *Crack Wars*, the theorist Avital Ronell asks, "What do we hold against the drug addict?" and answers her own question with a quote from Jacques Derrida: "That he cuts himself off from the world, in exile from reality, far from objective reality and the real life of the city and the community; that he escapes into a world of simulacrum and fiction . . . We cannot abide the fact that his is a pleasure taken in an experience without truth."

Blueschild Baby is an illumination of the deep misunderstandings lodged at the core of this case against the addict: George is an addict enmeshed in the world of his city, sculpted by the dreams and damage of his community, escaping nothing—seeking, more than anything, a reckoning with truth: the possible selves that might dwell inside him, underneath the stories that have turned him—alternately—into a savior and a villain.

* * *

When it was first published in 1970, *Blueschild Baby* effectively predicted Nixon's war on drugs a year before it officially began. Even as George struggles to overcome his addiction to heroin in these pages, he is fully aware of the ways his government wants to turn his addiction against him. "They say you're arrested for crime, narcotics, prostitution, robbery, murder, but these are not the reasons for locking you away," he thinks. In an interview conducted decades later, Nixon's domestic policy chief, John Ehrlichman, confessed to precisely this: "Did we know we were lying about the drugs?" he asked. "Of course we did." Ehrlichman said that the Nixon administration couldn't make it illegal to be black, but they could link the black community to heroin: "We could arrest their leaders, raid their homes, break up their meetings, and vilify them night after night on the evening news."

The plot of *Blueschild Baby* turns on a pivotal scene of shaming: When George goes to see a doctor for help in kicking his habit, he gets treated like a criminal. He's fresh from prison, where he served time for possession, and is deep in the throes of withdrawal. Even his vomit shows signs of struggle: "Live things, frogs and insects kick in the liquid coming out." When George's girlfriend, Nandy, suggests that he see a doctor, George knows better. He tells her, "A doctor won't help." And, sure enough, as soon as George tells the doctor he's a drug addict, the doctor immediately proves him right. He backs up from his desk and draws a pistol. The scene doesn't unfold as a conflict between men so much as a conflict between narratives of addiction that don't agree. George and Nandy insist on addiction as a disease—"He's a sick man, you're a doctor," Nandy says, and George insists, "I'm sick, in pain like anybody else that comes to you"—but the doctor and his gun won't surrender the notion of addiction as vice. He says: "Get out of my office before I call the police."

The addict has long been seen as someone fully to blame for his own wrecked life, and for his corrosive effects on his community. When Nancy Reagan launched her famous "Just Say No" campaign, in 1982, its slogan offered implicit recrimination: *Just say no* meant also *Some said yes*. As George H. W. Bush's National Drug Control Strategy would put it a decade later: "The drug problem reflects bad decisions by individuals with free wills."

This vision of the addict—as an agent of betrayal, undermining the shared social project—has been an enduring character in what the criminologist Drew Humphries calls the drug-scare narrative. It's a classic American genre that singles out a particular substance as cause for alarm—often arbitrarily, without an increase in use—in order to scapegoat a marginal community. Racial paranoia has been part of American drug-scare narratives for as long as they've been told, even though the majority of drug users have always been white. "NEGRO COCAINE 'FIENDS' NEW SOUTHERN MENACE," a *New York Times* headline ran, in 1914, and similar articles spread the myth of the black "fiend" as an almost supernatural enemy.

It happened not only with black cocaine use in the early twentieth century—fearmongering was used to drum up support for the 1914 Harrison Narcotics Tax Act, which regulated drugs for the first time—but with Chinese immigrants and opium in nineteenth-century California; with Mexicans and marijuana in the 1930s; with black heroin use in the 1950s; with the inner-city crack epidemic of the 1980s; with the rise of meth in poor white communities at the turn of the twenty-first century.

Every addiction story needs a villain. But America has never been able to decide whether addiction is an illness or a crime. Some addicts get pitied, others get blamed. Alcoholics are tortured geniuses. Drug addicts are deviant zombies. Male drunks are thrilling. Female drunks are bad moms. White addicts get their suffering witnessed. Addicts of color get punished. Celebrity addicts get tabloid headlines and posh rehab with equine therapy. Poor addicts get prison terms. Someone carrying crack cocaine gets five years, while someone driving drunk gets a night in jail, even though drunk driving kills more people every year than all illegal drugs combined. In her account of mass incarceration, *The New Jim Crow,* Michelle Alexander points out that many of these biases tell a much larger story about "who is viewed as disposable—someone to be purged from the body politic—and who is not."

* * *

When I started reading literary narratives of addiction, and absorbing literary mythologies of addiction, I was struck by how many of these works—and these myths—were by and about dead white men. The lineage of boozy luminaries, literary legends I worshipped as a young writer coming of age, ranged from the modernist drunks—Ernest Hemingway, William Faulkner, F. Scott Fitzgerald—to the sages who followed them across the course of the twentieth century: John Berryman, Malcolm Lowry, William Burroughs, John Cheever, Raymond Carver, David Foster Wallace. I'd always seen these authors as dashing rogues—appealingly dysfunctional silhouettes—who mined dark wisdom from the depths of their tormented psyches.

There are other accounts of addiction out there, of course, but many of their authors haven't made it into the canon: Clarence Cooper's 1967 novel, *The Farm,* an acutely realized portrait of addiction and "the cure" at a federal prison-hospital in Kentucky, and an astute dissection of the ways "rehabilitation" has often involved yet another assertion of white control over incarcerated men of color; Lee Stringer's 1998 memoir, *Grand Central Winter,* about his days of addiction and homelessness, and how he finally, literally, started to write his way out of them; and James Welch's 1974 novel, *Winter in the Blood,* about an alcoholic Blackfoot Indian in the midst of an existential crisis under the huge skies of Montana.

Blueschild Baby tells a very different story from the mythologies I'd inherited about dead white men who wrote beautiful prose—who turned their psychic pain into heavy drinking, heavy using, and iconic art. This novel excavates its fair share of dark wisdom, but it doesn't lean on any easy mythologies about the triangular relationship between suffering, addiction, and beauty. Instead, it tells the story of a man who has done hard time for his addiction because his country decided—before he was ever born—that he had probably already done something wrong.

The novel begins with George arriving back in Manhattan after his release from prison—even the sight of Manhattan makes him crave the drugs again—and follows him through a few increasingly desperate scores, through a grudging reunion with his former partner and four-year-old daughter, and then a meeting with his parole officer in the Newark courthouse—where he passes the "marks of rebellion" on Springfield Avenue, the residue of the recent riots: blackened stores and broken glass and a burnt smell in the air.

Nothing about this novel is easy. Its protagonist has more in common with the "unrepentant addict" of William Burroughs's *Junky* than with the uplifting heroes of more straightforward tales of recovery and redemption. Its protagonist is callous and abusive. George watches a woman overdose and feels mainly a kind of strange thrill at being able to pronounce her dead. He sees his four-year-old daughter for the first time since she was born, and then leaves her again. He feels little more than loathing for her mother. He sexually assaults her babysitter. Cain resists respectability politics at every turn—by presenting a character who is smart and full of yearning, but often acts aggressively, violently, even unthinkably.

In the novel, George explains himself as a black man sick of being touted as a trophy of racial upward mobility, worn out by John Henryism and tired of performing model citizenship. He is a former high-school basketball star and college scholarship kid who has ended up scoring drugs back in the same projects where he was raised. The novel is almost absurd in the extravagance of how Cain demonizes his fictional protagonist, after giving him his own name—as if Cain has made a hair shirt of his own novel, exaggerating his own sins and painting himself as villain in order to exorcise his own demons and to force his readers into contact with a character who is both wronged and wronging, difficult to root for—an addict who spends much of the book harming others.

How many times have I read certain scenes in this novel—when George watches a man rape an unconscious woman after her overdose and does not intervene; or when he forces himself on his daughter's young babysitter—and wished it existed without them? Many times. That would make it an easier novel, full of shapelier morals and guided by a more "likable" protagonist. The novel that exists is more vexing, more confounding, more conflicted in the responses it provokes—ultimately a more apt way of documenting addiction itself, a condition that often produces behaviors that alienate our sympathies at every turn. Someone doesn't need to be blameless, Cain suggests, in order to deserve human complexity on the page—in order to illuminate the tangled knot of addiction, and the subtleties of how we narrate its thrall.

This conflicted quality—in its many facets—is what ultimately makes *Blueschild Baby* a great work of art. This novel is alive to the truth of addiction as a socially constructed experience *and* a physically brutal ordeal. It's alive to the harms its narrator has suffered, *and* the many ways he has harmed others. It's alive to both the wonder and horror of its particular New York City, to the way the broad avenues of Harlem—its north-south thoroughfares—are festive and bustling, while its smaller east-west cross streets feel dilapidated and hopeless—a symbolic articulation of the ways a city can feel simultaneously awe-inspiring and soul-crushing.

Cain writes with his whole body. His prose is full of all five senses: glittering neon signs and the sick-sweet stench of a dealer's den; the tinkle of an ice cream truck and the rubbery spine of a heroin rush, the feel of cold eggs in the mouth after a long night. When I spoke to Cain's ex-wife, Jo Lynne Pool, years after the end of their marriage, she said that while he was working on the novel he carried his notebooks with him everywhere he went. (Even when he went uptown to score.) I can feel that *carried-them-everywhere*-ness in his prose—those notebooks traveling through the grit and particularity of the world, so he could transcribe not just vague notions of the world, but its exquisite and excruciating grain.

✳ ✳ ✳

About halfway through the novel, George runs into an old friend named Nandy, takes her to a jazz club, falls immediately in love and decides he wants to get clean for her. (His parole officer has also threatened to send him back to prison if he fails a urine test in seventy-two hours.) Across the course of the novel, George shifts away from the ways he'd once tried to justify his using to himself. He once understood it as a *fuck you* to the social order, a way "to live life unhindered" by rebelling against white power structures or the tyrannical demands of racial upward mobility. But later in the book, when George passes a crowd of "nodding junkies" on the street, listening to a man who is calling for support for "victims of the Newark rebellion," he sees them "no longer [as] the chosen driven to destruction by their awareness and frustration, but only lost victims, too weak to fight."

The arc of *Blueschild Baby* stages a conflict between various narratives of addiction—as political rhetoric, or a form of social rebellion—but it never forgets addiction as a bodily reality: jangling nerves and dry skin, gaunt bodies and sweat, the sensation of "bones scraping against one another inside." The novel closes on a note of tentative hope, with George recalling the first night he shot heroin—when "a strange moon hung in the sky" and he was first swallowed by that "calm, terribly sudden and infinite"— before he renounces it for good.

But this renunciation points to yet another tension embedded in the book—or at least, what it means to read the book now, almost fifty years after it was first published, now that its author has been dead nearly a decade: We know that the character of George Cain still believes in his ability to free himself from the same addiction that his author died from.

Just as Cain's novel resists fetishizing addiction as rebellion, refusing to ignore its human cost, Cain's own life thwarts the impulse to narrate self-awareness as salvation. Cain's lived addiction brought together several driving forces—the allure of the tortured artist spinning darkness into gold, and the stress of being a black man in a country that had cosigned on the notion of his criminality before he was born—but dissecting these motivations in his novel wasn't enough to liberate him from the physical imperatives of dependence itself. He was able to turn that addiction into powerful and provocative art, electrified by self-knowledge, but that brilliance—that insight, that deep awareness—wasn't enough to save him.

When I asked Cain's ex-wife if she ever tried to get him to stop using, she said simply, "I knew better."

* * *

When I first reached out to Jo Lynne Pool—through her and Cain's son, Malik, whom I had managed to track down—she was surprised that anyone still cared about her former husband. But I wanted to learn more about this man who had written a stunning, disturbing, singular book and then fallen into almost total obscurity, and she was glad to talk to me about his brilliance and his troubles.

Pool told me that Cain started shooting heroin after dropping out of college, operating under the notion—as she put it—that "writers needed conflict and adversity. So he deliberately went out to find some." After dropping out of Iona College, a Catholic school where he'd been given a basketball scholarship, Cain headed west through Texas, and eventually spent six months in a Mexican jail on marijuana charges. When he got out of jail, Pool said, "he had the makings of a book."

By the time Pool first met him, in the late sixties, he was already a full-blown addict, though Pool didn't realize it. She'd come from Texarkana to study at Pratt, and she'd never met "a dope fiend, or a heroin addict, or any other kind of addict." She was immediately drawn to Cain, with his "green snake eyes" and his evident and overwhelming intelligence. He always walked around with two or three composition books tucked under his arm.

After Pool and Cain had their first child, he lived two lives. In one, he was trying to be a more present father. He became a Sunni Muslim and joined a mosque that was like a surrogate family. But he would also disappear for days at a time—go up to Harlem (notebooks in tow) and come back glazed. He'd nod out in the middle of dinner. One time, he had a few friends over and while Pool was in the bathroom his friends took off with half her clothes and armfuls of their baby supplies. Cain had to chase them down the street to get it all back. In the *New York Times* review of *Blueschild Baby*, Addison Gayle Jr. interprets Cain's recovery story as a narrative of racial self-possession, as he redeems himself in the "72 hours of living hell" that constitute his withdrawal. "In that time," Gayle writes, "George Cain, former addict, emerges phoenix-like from the ashes, as George Cain, black man." In this interpretation, sobriety—rather than addiction—becomes the way he resists white oppression.

The publication of *Blueschild Baby* brought Cain the buzz and affirmation he had been craving—the sense of arrival. His publisher, McGraw-Hill, threw him a party in a beautiful loft in Soho. A few days after getting his first royalty check, he ran into one of his friend's little brothers on the street, took him to a record store nearby, and told him to choose all the records he wanted. Cain and Pool had James Baldwin over for dinner. "People assume black women can cook, so I had to figure out how to fry chicken," Pool told me. Everyone loved the book; Cain's mother was only disappointed that she couldn't recommend it to her friends from church. The affirmation of this reception quieted something in Cain—and for a few years, at least, he was using less.

But by the time he got a temporary appointment at the Iowa Writers' Workshop—on the merits of the book and its success, moving to Iowa City with Pool and their infant daughter—Cain was restless. He started flying back to New York every weekend. When Pool told him they couldn't afford his commutes, he took a bus to Davenport—about an hour away, right by the Mississippi—and didn't come back for days. Eventually, Pool took a bus there herself, with their baby in tow, and when she asked a cabbie to take her to the junkie part of town, he pulled up to a run-down building where she found George inside and "dragged him out by his ear."

Back in Brooklyn, after his temporary appointment at Iowa was over, Cain kept trying to commit himself to a second novel. He didn't want to fall into the "one and only" trap to which he thought so many black writers had succumbed. He was using more because his writing wasn't going well, and his writing wasn't going well because of all his using. He was juggling a full-time teaching gig at Staten Island Community College and a full-time addiction; an infant son in addition to his young daughter. For Pool, their marriage ended the night she picked up the phone and heard a woman tell her that she was pregnant with Cain's child. Pool left Cain without telling him where she was going, and ended up moving to Houston with their two kids. After years, Cain found them and came out to visit. But he didn't like it there. "The sky was too open," Pool told me. "He felt like God could see him."

When she spoke to me about Cain, Pool's voice was full of respect and even tenderness. It was clear she'd been through a lot with him, *for* him, but she didn't regret it. She mainly regretted how his life had turned out. He died in poverty, his work basically unknown. She told me about his last apartment, in Harlem, where their kids went—just once, as teenagers—to stay. It was a basement unit that smelled like sewage.

When we spoke, Pool told me that the mutual friend who had introduced them felt guilty about connecting a "pure-souled country girl" to a Harlem junkie, but she told him there was nothing to apologize for. "How many people get to cook chicken for James Baldwin?" she asked me. In our conversations about Cain, she used the word *genius* more times than I could count. She wasn't bitter about their marriage. She'd just done what she had to do. "I'm not upset," she told me. "I just needed to make sure we survived George."

They did survive George, and so did this novel. The only person who didn't survive George was George himself—who could not ultimately liberate himself from the addiction he documented so unsparingly in these pages. One of the most powerful ways you can honor his memory is to read them.

LESLIE JAMISON, 2018

I

IT IS GETTING DARK NOW and still I roam the corridors of bedlam. I need sanctuary, but there is none, and as my invisibility leaves like a cloak, I feel naked, center of all eyes, fair game for whoever first stumbles across me. I'm at 63rd on Amsterdam and must make it to 81st Street, past the Red Cross on 66th, faggots' 72nd and the police station on 68th. They are loosing our warders, changing shifts like changing of the guard, and they come streaming in a blue mass. The squat police station vomiting them up, armed with clubs, the majority's arrogance and a .38. They cruise the alleys and byways of this place looking to snatch us up, kill us if we resist. See me, all crouch and stealth, slipping softly toward a corner, well lit by a *bodega,* all the while expecting the shouted "Halt!" or fatal bullet from behind. Turn a corner and out of sight, restraining muscles bursting to break in violent activity and carry me off. Walking, one step, two, never turning, as if not seeing them will prevent their seeing me. Then looking, I see nothing, they are beyond the corner or maybe never were.

A sickness comes over me in this twilight state, somewhere between wake and sleep, my nose runs and my being screams for heroin. It is an internal nervous disorder which floods the brain and shortcircuits senses. I infect the world with it.

I try to halt the parade of images, it is to no avail. They continue as if no part of self. I am growing smaller, vanishing, the world negating me. Made midget by canyon-forming structures looking down from inanimity. A clicked heel sounds loud in quiet, then echoes to silence. Sounding more often, still silence its dominant theme. Unable to diminish the rest between beats and I'm running fast as I can. My image runs out of the evening, a dusk-colored mauve, setting city sun at my back, to collide with me then vanish at moment of impact, image made counterfeit by countless repetitions thrown from vacant windows. Buildings pass in rapid succession of sameness, each as the other. To stranger's eyes, dirty brownstones bearing no marks of difference, but to me, Georgie Cain, each is unique, bearing personality vested in and by me.

I come to Sun's building. Looking over my shoulder to be sure I am not followed, I dash in. They're posed as always, the other inmates of bedlam, pimps and prostitutes, the junky souls. Gracing the stairs like debutantes at the ball, all piled on one another, they stare vacantly into the well. Not in white gowns. Somber hued tatters the fashion. As I approach they salute me as comrades do, "Hey brother," and the bitches, "Baby." We are a fraternity of selflessness, bound together by our communal rejection. We love each other and know it not.

I'm hesitant, nervous before my audience with the king. The room is silent, but they are in there. I smell them. Bright Sun and Flower, fearfully frozen behind the door awaiting identification. Friend or foe. So long have they lived in this room, it stinks of them and leaks into the hall. Sulphur, cigarettes and decaying flesh, a stench so moist and clinging, no amount of air can dispel it.

It is the smell of the dead season, fall, in a Texas penitentiary.

One knew the season had changed, the death of the fall was then. But there was no slow diminution of summer. One day it was summer and the next, fall full-grown. No change in weather, no browning or falling leaves to tell me. But the crickets were dead and dying, and only a day before I had kicked them up at every step filling air with their raucous cry and answer. Then they lay heaped upon the ground, small forms dotting the earth like dried balls of clay flung from a turning wheel. Their decomposition fouled the air. A heavy yellow mist, fetid and rotten, rose from them. I breathed it in, tasting on my palate, in my stomach and wanted to vomit. Sun's room smells the same and betrays his presence. I knock softly and Flower queries. "Who?"

"Georgie."

"It's Georgie, Sun."

"Well let him in woman."

As always, Sun is holding court, surrounded by his motley crew of buffoons and servants who perform for him and carry out an occasional order, stick a knife in a back or go to the store for eats. Their only reward, the shelter of this room and an occasional fix. From his throne, the always unmade bed, Sun carries on the business of his kingdom. I am a black knight-errant whose fealty is desired, so am summoned to sit beside him. Flower is his woman, the reigning queen, she is dangerous and carries a switchblade to protect her man. Who would expect the knife from that quarter, comely black child of innocence? She is lately out of the hospital, suffering from tuberculosis and heroin.

I ask her health. "How you doing Flow?"

"Okay Georgie. Was sick awhile with TB, just got out the hospital. Signed myself out. They wanted me to stay six months. Couldn't stand it any longer, so I came on back. On the welfare now, got an apartment on Ninety-seventh Street. I just come by to be with Sun awhile. We're not supposed to be together. So they give him an apartment downtown here and me one uptown. But I stay down here with Sun and we go up there when we get tired."

Overcome for a moment, she pauses and nods, then continues. "I'm feeling good though, but that's only cause I got out. I need these streets, they're in my blood. I'm okay long as I can run these streets with Sun. Then everything's okay, don't feel no pain, junk takes care of that. Cough and spit blood every now and then, but it ain't nothing."

Tired of his lady's monologue, Sun silences her with a gesture and turns to me. His head is monumental with close-cropped, deeply receding hair, features strongly Indian and broken nose. The joke is, such a head on that gnome's body. He can barely carry it about he is so short and hunched over. He whispers so the others in the room cannot hear. "How many do you want?" From somewhere deep in his pants fly he pulls out the plastic wrapped packets of bags and hands me three. I give Flow the money and reaching into her bosom she pulls forth crumpled bills and views them strangely for a moment as if she were surprised at their appearance. Recovering, she adds mine to the pile and shows her hollow breasts as she replaces them, then moves to the window and draws the shade.

"Why don't you get off here? Know you don't feel like running the streets with stuff on you." Sun has planted a seed bursting in my brain, returned is my fear of the police. I cannot walk the streets with heroin in my possession, it distorts my posture, making me furtive and sneaking, unable to meet anyone's eye. This is the curse of Cain, not to have committed crime and yet burdened with guilt.

"Flow get my things out, Georgie's going to get off."

She rummages in a box overflowing with clothes and finding the apparatus, sets it up on the table.

I dump the stuff in the cooker, add water, cook, and tie up.

Then draw most of the solution into the dropper. I plunge it into my arm, apopping and crackling as it tears through old scar tissue, then the click of a punctured vein and I squeeze the bulb. There is no longer anything dramatic or pleasurable about junk, it is only medicine, a restorative to enable me to function. It is done and the world returns to normal. Inanimate objects in the room no longer try to impose themselves upon me as had happened in the street, they are passive now, awaiting an aggressive consciousness to affirm their reality. My sickness has left, it is like waking. Rising from his bed, Sun walks to the cooker to see how well I've paid him. Junk is the coin of this realm, money is only the labor to acquire it. He is satisfied and draws it up. There is a lull in the world, a comfortable peace, all is still for a moment. Lack of heroin insulated me from the sounds and activities, but now awareness comes.

Head buried between her legs, gagging on spit, Tracy screams across the room. "Georgie today's my birthday, I'm nineteen years old. We're having a party, right momma?"

"That's right baby," Flow answers.

"Come and kiss me Georgie."

"Kiss her for her birthday," urges Sun, and I move to do so intending to cheek her, instead she grabs my head and presses her lips to mine, choking me with tongue and saliva.

"A birthday kiss. Don't try and fuck her," laughs Sun.

"Leave her go," slobbers the white boy, awake now in the corner. Letting her go, I fall back on the bed.

"Tommy wake up," Tracy calls to him. "Meet Georgie."

"Hey man." Words stumble from his mouth guttural and moist. All the while he struggles to keep his head up and eyes open.

"Don't I know you Georgie? Damn it's hot in here, open the windows Sun."

"They're open."

"Take your shirt off," suggests Flow, and he strips to his pants and begins picking his toes, sweating like a pig. His white skin is covered with tattoos and shines like plastic. It is hot, and I take my shirt off and begin tearing my flesh, leaving long fingernail trails across my skin and an open wound here and there that bleeds freely. I scratch an itch as if it were the most gratifying act in the world, deriving the utmost satisfaction from it, physical and mental. The dope makes you itch and nod. Nodding as if your spine were rubber, with closed lids. Closed lids signify your closing off the world and turning inside to find and order the chaos about you. We're all sitting shut up in this room, shut up in ourselves.

"How's the stuff?" asks Sun.

"Nice, real nice."

"Thought you'd go for it. I knew you'd be by tonight. Told Flow, Georgie'd be by to score. You hooked again?"

"Don't know, haven't stopped to find out."

"Still working?"

"Yeah."

"Don't know how you do it. You need to give this shit up and go on back to school. When I heard you were fucken around, couldn't believe it. Georgie Cain, the intellect, big time basketball star, it was a bitter pill baby. How long ago was that?"

"Five years Sun."

"Yeah, five years. Been a long time. How old are you now, twenty-one, two?"

"Twenty-two."

"You'd be playing pro ball and teaching now. You always said you wanted to teach."

I hate when they talk of my past as if I were a failure, I'm still alive and that is more important than any success, there is more than one way of dying and I was dying horribly. There was no me, only bits and pieces of everything and everybody, bound and tied to a whole race of people, black people, obligated to die and suffer making it for them. They don't see my addiction in its proper perspective. My need to live life unhindered, with no ties. The only way was to be rejected by those who respected and loved me, then I could begin anew. The process is nearly complete. Someday soon, I shall emerge as Georgie Cain.

"I still want to teach."

"Why don't you go on back to school? You could make it."

"Been thinking about it, but I don't have it any more."

"Don't have it! Shit. You're only twenty-two, your whole life is still ahead. You're only a kid. If I were your age and knew what you know, I'd have it made. I remember when you first showed on the set, you were a fucked-up cat, always talking from the books, but now you've lived some, you know what it's all about, and combined with all your knowledge, you can make it."

"I'm like Flower, Sun. These streets got me, I'm hooked."

"You know Georgie, this dope thing used to be a hell of a game, it was worth the hassle, when you had cats like Cicki Bones and his brothers putting junk on the street. The scag was boss and the time was light. They didn't fuck with you much then. But now they call it the dying game. I'm in it cause I can't do nothing else, welfare ain't enough to live off. I want, need, like every motherfucker out there and this is the only way I can do it. Whitey wasn't letting me go to school or teaching us nothing then. But you kids got it made today. They're begging for niggers to come and do things."

There it is again, they all want you to be a martyr, cloaking it in the guise of personal success, you can make it nigger if you try and the price is loneliness, because when you make it, you ain't black no more and you ain't white, somewhere in between.

"Momma I love you," moans Tracy.

"I know baby, I know," Flower answers.

"Ain't that a bitch. She calls Flow momma. Flow black as coal and she whiter than white, and she really means it. She and Flow live together. Kind of take care of each other. Flow's sick and Tracy keeps an eye on her."

"Yeah Georgie, we take care of each other, Tracy and me."

"No, no!" Tommy screams from a nod.

Tracy shakes him awake. "What's the matter? You dreaming again? God damn. You're getting to be a pain in the ass, always screaming. You ain't in the joint no more."

"I'm sorry baby, can't help it. I'll get over it."

"I hope so. He's like that all night. When we're at Flow's, he keeps us up with all his screaming and shit. I love momma and she needs rest. You with your noise all night, I don't know what they did to you in that place."

"Yeah, Tracy takes care of Flow." The junk is having its effect, Sun is repeating himself, soon he'll be off the bed and into his little dance and Flower will sing, the king and queen will perform for me.

"We take care of each other, Tracy and me. Listen, dig how I met her. Was coming out the building one day and the cop had her in the hall asking for identification and whatnot. You can see she's only a kid. Guess he thought she was a runaway or something, I'd seen her around the block, knew she'd fucked around, but we'd never said nothing. Anyway, I walk up to her and I say what's wrong baby and she says, 'Momma, this policeman . . .' The cop, he don't even let her finish, but turns and looks at my black face, then her white one and back to me again and says, 'Is this your daughter.' I say, 'Yes she's my daughter.' I'd just come out the hospital then, was looking healthy and had some decent clothes on. He just shakes his head and says, 'Well she shouldn't be out so late,' and walks off. We been together ever since."

"That's something, ain't it," mumbles Sun. "Wish I could've been there to see the cat's face."

The white boy tries again. "Don't I know you Georgie?"

"No I don't think so."

Feeling me tense, Sun tries to ease the situation. "Georgie just got back."

"I just got out the joint myself, Monday. Did a nickel at Attica. Five calendars, it was a bitch."

Why doesn't he carry a sign around his neck, telling the world? He and Sun are thinking that having done time, there is the common ground, a meeting place and this will ease the tension. It's like the other niggers in the joint who called me brother, automatically assuming because I was black, having shared the experience of blackness, we were closer than say two other people meeting for the first time. But it ain't so, a black is as treacherous as a white, all bear watching and familiarity does breed contempt.

"Tracy's my woman, last time I saw her, she was a little kid." Extending his arm, he shows me how little. "She used to hang with my kid sister. I hit the bricks Monday and I'm out hunting a fix and who do I run into but her. She scores for me and we all got straight, me, her and Flower. Flow's a good woman, she got big heart, but Tracy surprised the shit out of me."

"Tommy you got money?" Tracy asks.

"No baby, I'm busted."

"Tommy it's my birthday. I want to get fucked-up."

"You're fucked-up now baby, you don't need no more jive."

"Tommy you got money?"

"I told you no."

"Tommy buy me a bag, please baby."

"I ain't got no money."

"You stingy cocksucker, I know that faggot you screwed gave you some money. After all I did for you, you won't even buy me a bag. Dig this creep, will you. Flow and I pick him off the streets, let him flop at the pad, score for him, bring him here to Sun's and he don't want to buy no dope. Tommy please, it's my birthday, don't do me this way, I'm nineteen today, I'll get you the money back tomorrow. You know I will."

Reaching out, he pulls her from the chair. "Bitch what's wrong with you?" And they stare into each other, both incapable of any real emotion or violence. They are dead, even her scathing retort was mumbled in toneless monologue. His anger was only a polite query. Releasing her he feels in his pocket and pulls out bills, counting them he puts one in his pocket and passes the rest to Sun.

"It's your birthday baby, so we're going to celebrate. Have a party." He reaches over and turns the radio on. "Sun give me six bags. Flow get the works, I'm turning everybody on." There is a great commotion to oblige and Tracy hollers, "First!" She smooths hair from her forehead and lights a cigarette. Proud of her power and arrogant. They cook the junk up and we all get off. Flow cleans the works, stashes them, then sits on the bed next to Sun and begins nodding. Sun gets up from the bed and without a word begins dancing in time with the music, a swaying and bending low. Like a snake being charmed, his grotesque body moves fluidly beneath the beautiful head and tells a story. It's a mad man's mime, with steps slow-moving, drug-hindered, a falling low. This must have been the dominant medium, before the invention and limitations of speech. He tells of his blackness and bares a soul. Tommy never having seen this performance is embarrassed by its frankness and turns away. Tracy is high and uncaring. She is still and her fingernails are turning blue. Flower watches his every move as I do. There is his childhood, the marriage to Flower, the prisons, the police, the dope, his wanting what every other motherfucker wants. All this he tells in a dance. With a gesture a million empty words are spare, and he would give up his sotted

life for mine, if he could. The music stops and he is frozen in las-
situde, sweat runs from every pore staining his clothes and falls
to the floor. He is no longer with us, but somewhere in vastness,
rushing past the moon and stars, bumping against time and space,
an instrument, not a will of his own, in some unknown hand. He
is poised but a moment and crashes to the floor, groveling about
and slobbering like an epileptic. Tommy frightened rushes from
his chair to help and Flower has a knife at his throat.

"Don't touch him, don't touch him." She raises the gnome, lays
the noble head cross her lap, rocking and singing in a voice tired-
toned and weeping, sounding like Billie. She is a bitch singing
love to her man. Tommy looks to me for enlightenment.

Tracy is out and dying of narcotic poison. The blueness is stealing up her fingers and air passes gently through her open mouth,
no one notices it but me.

"What's happening?"

Flower stops singing and cuts her eyes at him as if he'd committed heresy. I wave him silent making him understand everything is all right. He falls back in his chair and closing his eyes
begins scratching his crotch. Flower resumes singing in her blues
voice the piece playing on the radio and Tracy is dying. Flower
sings well enough to be a professional, but she is old and no one
but us will ever hear her.

Sun is awake now and stares at the ceiling. Flow sings softly
in his ear and he smiles. Footsteps sound in the outside hall and
she reaches over and turns the radio off, gesturing us to silence.
Tracy cannot make a sound, the bitch is dying. Someone comes
up to the door, hesitates, then retreats, stops, approaches again
and then knocks. Sun pushes Flower from the bed and sends her
to the door.

"Who?"

"Santo," comes the muffled reply.

"Santo, I don't know no Santo. See what he wants," says Sun.

"What do you want?"

"Is Sun there?"

"What do you want?"

"Give me three."

She cracks the door. "Oh. It's you. It's Saint, Sun."

"Tell him to wait a minute."

"Just a minute Saint."

Sun goes digging in his fly and brings up three bags. Flower takes the money, then passes the dope out through the crack. She locks the door and pushes a chair against it. Puts the money with the rest, pats it in place and returns to bed.

Tommy pulls his chair across from Tracy and sits facing her, holding the dead hands. He can't open his eyes and struggles to stay conscious. Leaning forward to kiss her lips, he misses, banging against her. The limp head flies over the back of the chair and hangs like the neck is broken. He puts his hand on her breasts. Even near death, she moves slightly to elude him. He leans over her like some strange beast and tries to kiss her lips again, but the head rolls crazily and will not be still. His hands go to her crotch and she doesn't move. His face contorts with lust and rage, he tries to kiss her but the elusive head will not oblige. He is red and running short of breath, slaps her and the sound raises us. Seeing the dead girl, Flower screams and pulls her blade forcing Tommy to the corner.

"What the fuck is wrong with you? Why didn't you say something? She's taken an O.D." Turning to Tracy, begins slapping her to bring her around. But it is late. There are blue circles under her eyes.

"You up here trying to fuck and she's dying. What kind of man are you? You ain't shit, what did they do to you in the joint? Should've kept your ass in there."

Fear has cleared his head and made him alert. "I didn't know."

"Yeah, you just got out the joint, you wouldn't. You're practically out yourself. Don't stand there. Wet that washcloth and hand it to me. Georgie get the ice out the box."

Sun sits on the bed mumbling. "Oh shit, that bitch better not die in my room, all those fools in the hall. We'll never get her out of here." Moving from the bed, he hunts his works from their hiding place and prepares a salt shot. Flower mops Tracy's brow then her breasts, she doesn't stir. I feel for her pulse, there is none. "She is dead." I say it and am thrilled by my pronouncement, how many of us can pronounce a person dead? She is the first person I've ever seen die. Sun shoots her up with salt, she doesn't move, but there is an ugly hole where he gave the injection. He is beating and boxing her ears, but the head only rolls limply from side to side. Flower takes ice and puts it between her breasts till they freeze white, then strips her and lays the body on the bed. She isn't proud or arrogant now, but rather childish and vulnerable. I do want her to live and silently I utter all the prayers I've ever heard. Flow jams ice between her thighs in the pubic hair, then pushes it up her pussy.

"Georgie, massage her breasts."

"I'll do it," says Tommy.

"No. You sit the fuck down and keep out the way."

We administer to her naked corpse for hours, till we are covered in sweat from fear and exertion, and still she's just as when we started.

"Let me try artificial respiration," says Tommy.

"You might as well have your way with her, she'll never know," says Flow, angry now, not so much at Tracy's dying but the inconvenience it will cause. Dying is a common occurrence, it's the name of the game.

He put his lips on hers, his naked chest against her, and blew his breath in her, he did it for ten, twenty, thirty minutes, an hour or more and nothing. He kissed her as if she weren't dead, strangling her with spit, rolling his body against hers and rousing himself to coming. His kisses were so strong, almost substance, the denial of five years fled his mouth to hers, seeming to warm the room. He made love, whispering, eliciting from himself some vestige of life to pass into her. Worded passion, a hymn he sang.

"Baby come on out of it," he chanted.

"The greedy bitch, had to be first. Told her not to try and shoot it all." Could hear Sun in the back, pacing. "Maybe we can take her out over the fire escapes?"

"Baby come on, ain't nothing wrong with you. You just want some attention. You ain't no little kid no more baby, come on wake up." He smacked her across the face and rode her up and down moving her body to suit his movements. Fucking her he began again the fervid chant. Riding her belly he prayed like a zealot at the cross.

"Baby wake up. You know ain't nothing wrong. Just want some attention, you ain't no little shit ass are you. You ain't no little shit ass baby, wake up. You're a big girl now. I'm your old man, ain't I your old man. Baby don't do this to me. Wake up baby. Please wake up," he begged. "Baby don't do me this way. I need you. This is your man talking to you baby. You're my woman, ain't you my woman." His voice was soft and caressing, "Baby we got too many things to do together, you can't cut out on me like this."

Sun and Flower stood conferring in the corner how they could best dispose of the body and I sat in the chair paralyzed by what went on.

She hiccupped and rolled, protesting his rape and we ran to the bed, Flower pulled him off and began beating Tracy about the breasts. She hiccupped some more, bringing up bile and began moaning softly. Flower got the ice and administered it to the vital areas and she began breathing. He'd loved her into life, Tommy had, with my eyes I saw him do it. He sat in the chair, overcome, spent, there was nothing in him, he looked drained of life and dead.

Flow threw a sheet over Tracy and put her in the tub, we could hear the cold water running through the pipes. When they came back into the room Flower supported Tracy. She shivered and still blue in the lips, sat on the bed. "Anyone got a smoke?"

I lit one and handed it to her.

"How long have I been out?"

"About four hours," Sun said.

Then Tommy began. "We had a hell of a time bringing you back, ice, salt shot, artificial respiration, took your clothes off . . ."

She cut him short. "You finally got what you wanted. Uh. You bastard."

A COCK CROWING IN THE CHICKEN HOUSE downstairs wakes me. So strange this rural outburst in the midst of the city it seems a fragment of dreams. A clothesline squeaks being drawn in, cans rattle somewhere, someone putting garbage out, a child screams at withheld breasts. The sounds travel in the lazy morning through the airshaft. Picture families sitting politely to breakfast. Moving from my chair, I walk to the window. Picture in black and white a frozen time and place, the city wrapped in morning haze. An early morning street strange in desertion, naked gray asphalt, unpeopled, running its length to the dirty green river which I cannot see but know is at all pavements' end.

I'm sick. My stomach sucks the body juices to a point below the navel where they gurgle merrily. My stomach contracting draws into a knot squeezing the eyeballs from my head and air from my ass, feel the cramps that will kick the bile from my guts coming on. I try to wake Sun.

"Sun, Sun. Wake up man."

He moves slowly and I shake him harder. His protestations wake Flow and she watches warily.

"Flow help me get him up."

"What for?"

"I want a fix."

"You give me a taste if I get the stuff for you?"

"I'll give you something."

"Leave him alone before he wakes up, I got it."

Reaching into her bosom, she pulls out the packet of bags. I give her the money, cook the solution and draw it into the spike. Looking in the cooker, she says, "Ain't nothing here. Thought you were going to leave me something."

"Look I'm sick Flow. You just got out the hospital, ain't nothing wrong with you."

"Yeah but if Sun were awake, you'd have to give him a taste."

"But Sun ain't awake."

She turns away for a moment, and while she isn't looking, stick my finger in the water jar and shake the drops into the cooker then pretend to squeeze a few from the spike in and look at her with disgust.

"Here. You're too much. You ain't got no habit."

She hits herself, waits for a rush then asks, "Do you feel it?"

"It's nice."

"I don't feel it too tough."

"How long you been out the hospital Flow?"

"Almost a month."

"Shit, you probably got a jones by now. I left you a nice taste. You should feel something."

"Feel it, but it just don't feel like last night."

I'm high, but pretend to be higher and after watching me a while, she convinces herself.

"Yeah, I feel it now, the stuff is nice. When Sun wakes, don't tell him I sold you two bags. Don't say you gave me a taste."

I feel myself returning to normal and watch her clean the works. We are straight now, filled with new energy, it's impossible to go to sleep. Walk to the window while she cleans the room. Picking rags and clothes off the floor, she begins sweeping, filling the air with dust.

"What the fuck you doing," Sun mumbles, choking awake.

"I'm cleaning," she says, gagging on dust and TB.

"Well sit down, you can do it later. What time is it Georgie?"

"Don't know."

Coming to the window, he looks upstreet to the clock in the check cashing place and mutters, "Nine o'clock."

"I gave you the stuff last night, didn't I Flow? How many bags we got left?"

Pulling the package from her blouse she counts carefully. "Four."

"Fix our shot while I wash," and he crosses to the basin while she cooks up.

"Who came by while I was out?"

"Nobody."

"What happened to the two bags then?"

"Oh, that's right. Ray came by and got two."

"Put them all in there, going to turn Georgie on." Turning to me he asks, "What you doing today Georgie?"

"Nothing. Why?"

"Feel like hanging out?"

"Yeah."

"Good, you can go uptown to re-up with me."

We are sitting around the table hitting ourselves when Tracy and Tommy wake. Watching us they tense with anticipation. Both are still high from last night but they begin sniffing and acting sick.

"What's the matter with you," Sun asks Tommy. "You can't be sick, you just got out here."

"Leave me a taste momma," Tracy begs Flow.

"I can't baby."

"Just a cotton. Please."

"I can't baby, got it in my arm already," and she boots the blood smiling. We finish up and clean the joints.

"Say Sun. Do me a favor? Let me cop two bags for a nickel, and I'll give you the rest later?"

"I would if I could Tommy, but I'm getting ready to go uptown to cop now. If you're still here when we get back I'll do it for you."

"How long you gonna be?"

"Going up now. If I find my man, be back in less than an hour, if I don't we'll have to shop around a while."

"We'll wait for you, but you'll do that for me?"

"I said I would. Give me the money Flow."

He stands counting it, eyes closed and lips moving computing something in his head. "Give me that nickel you got now Tommy."

"What for?"

"You want me to do you that favor don't you? Well I'm short and need cab fare."

He hands it over and Sun adds it to the rest. I hear Flow bolt and lock the door as we descend the stairs.

Exiting into the day, we walk toward Amsterdam Avenue, the clock in the check cashing place says 9:30. Winos shivering in a doorway beg the needed pennies for their medicine, another pukes, some young kids stand watching. They are tearing up the street to lay pipe and the trench crossing the avenue is covered with steel plate. A group of junkies idle in a doorway. Saturday morning.

There is nothing unusual about the car, but my eyes fix and watch it approach. A loud noise and its forward motion is abruptly reversed throwing the driver through the windshield. A woman screams. People come rushing forward. Two men struggle with the door and pretend to aid the victim. Sirens come wailing from downtown, the two break from the smoke carrying a woman's handbag. The police arrive and pull the woman from the car and lay her in the street. Curious we walk past the body, its face is blood, there are two raw holes where eyes should be. I feel sick. A cop combing the crowd for witnesses asks, "Nobody see what happened here? How about you buddy, you see what happened?"

Sun nods no. As we walk toward Broadway, he says, "Did you see that shit, fucken metal plate flipped up and cracked the axle, bitch went right through the window."

It is early and Broadway is just opening. Fruit vendors hosing down walks and store owners push steel gates from plate windows. We walk into the subway and stand on the platform. Scag runs in our veins and we feel it by bobbing and weaving. Squares stare, mistaking us for common drunks, we ignore them from the height of our state. Scag inflates you and you seem larger than life, above and outside it. The train comes. We enter and stand scratching and playing with our privates. People think us crude and dirty, in public, scratching our asses like low animals.

Two more junkies sit across from us. I felt their presence the moment we entered. I can always recognize a junky, no matter how clean or well disguised he is. If the President was one I and every other junky would know immediately. It is that faculty which enables all outcast types and renegades to recognize themselves. Sun and I and the two across the aisle are joined in conspiracy against the world. Though we don't know them, we are bound to them. Just as we are aware of them, they know and feel us in the same manner. Coming from a nod, one looks up and we gaze at each other emanating rays that inform us of the other. They're probably going to score too, our route, the Seventh Avenue Express to 116th Street is a well known and traveled one. We come to our station and Sun elbows me awake.

Coming from the pit, I'm blinded by the brilliant light of day. So bright it sears my eyes and I swoon, overcome. Cringing I clutch the banister.

"Something wrong?" Unable to speak I nod no. We've arrived in Harlem, land of black people, dead people, my people. A million sensations assail the senses making me stupid as an idiot, want to scream and halt the madness but only silence issues forth. Lenox Avenue is jammed and there is the perpetual air of carnival and party. Looking about me and seeing nothing but black people I am filled with a passionate love for them all. Something inside me kindles and reawakens, feel alive for the first time in ages. My junky spirit walks the street recognizing and recognized by other kindred spirits. They hail Sun and me and walking past, hawk their wares in whispers. Double-O-Seven, Green Power, Goldfinger, Sherry's Thing. One has bombidas for sale, another spikes, syringes and droppers, all the paraphernalia necessary to get straight. 117th Street and Lenox is an open air drug market. Two white bulls in plain-clothes sitting in a car are under surveillance by the crowds.

Sun is an oldtime dealer and convict, well known in these parts. Acquaintances come up to him to make sales and ask favors. He turns them away by telling them he ain't doing nothing. Sun spots someone half a block away and smiling taps me and points to him, it's his son, Broadway. I haven't seen him in years but heard he was in prison. Sun bounces up to him and delighted at seeing each other, they stand kissing and hugging unashamed.

"When did you raise?"

"Three weeks ago."

"Why didn't you get in touch with Flower and me, she'd be glad to see you."

"I didn't know where you lived, you changed your address, sent you a letter from the joint but it came back."

"Damn you look good. You know me and Flow back together. What you been doing since you got out? Fucking around again?"

"Yeah, light weight though, ain't got no jones yet."

Turning to me Sun says, "Broadway you remember Georgie, don't you?"

"Yeah you were a kid last time I saw you. Heard you'd got flagged. What you doing now?"

"Same old, same old," I reply.

With the amenities over, Sun begins taking care of business, who has got what and the quality of the dope on the street.

"Whose stuff you have today?" he asks Broadway.

"Had Jericho's thing."

"How is it?"

"Garbage, hardly turned my stomach over."

"How's the Fat Man's bag, it was dynamite last time I copped."

"No, it fell off. Goldfinger's got a boss bag out, only thing is he's got imitators and you can't be sure if it's his stuff."

"What do you mean?"

"You know how he seals his bags with that gold tape to let you know it's his thing? Well the minute cats got hip that he had the best thing on the street, they all started putting gold tape on their bags."

"How about Pee Wee, Sherry's, or Double-O?"

"All of them are boss, you can cop in the middle of the block off that chick. You know her name."

"You mean that fat black broad?"

"Yeah, she got all their things."

Reaching for a cigarette, Broadway pushes his jacket back and I see the stock of a sawed-off shotgun stuck in his belt.

"Dig Broadway, here's our address," and Sun scribbles it on a match cover. "Come down and see Flower, she be glad to see you."

"Okay. Later Sun," and he saunters away.

"Let's go into the block." On the way, Sun greets and waves to a hundred people. The avenues in Harlem have a festive air, but it is the streets that reveal the true nature of the place. Turning off into one is like entering hell. In these valleys, even nature seems more harsh.

A sun hung high makes soft tar and bakes the cement. Radiating heat waves shimmer on air, monkeys the children call them, they dance on air like the ten-cent string-controlled monkeys in the dime store. Light falls between the buildings, bright and stark, shadow forming, showing dirt encrusted brownstone, flaking fire escapes, piled scattered litter. Stray dogs, children, running and playing fill the streets with noise. But it is the air that lies over all hot and humid like some soft, giving casement that infects me and all those here. Air charged with a suppressed urgency, making you feel that at any moment all hell must break loose, a brawl, killing, anything. React by coiling myself, walking loose and almost dancing down street. Ready to flee or fight. Feel a strength and dignity unusual in me. I have no control or will but am prey to the capricious atmosphere, it is dynamic, having a presence of its own, apart from light or dark, still or moved. This isn't the same air and light I breathe and see in downtown. Walk down a street lined with black faces bearing the common expression, anger mingled with despair and I feel comfortable as I never do downtown.

Sun spots the woman across the street, she waves to us and we cross over.

"How you doing Sun?"

"Okay."

"How's Flower?"

"She just got out the hospital."

"Yeah, I know, she and I did time together."

"You straight?"

"Yeah, what you want?"

"Two halves."

"Walk into the hall."

We enter the dark hall and the stink of life overwhelms me, a stink of human waste and stale cooking, but over all this, the warm wonderful scent of sweated close-packed man.

I was born in a place like this. Remember a lumpy basketball spinning crazily downstreet pursued by a young horde and retrieved by me. Racing upstreet, hurled it through the fire escape rungs for a score. Nana, my grandmother, called me from her windowed perch. Feigning deafness continued playing till someone tapped my shoulder and pointed to her. The game was up then and entering the hall, gave a whistle to let her know I was coming.

"Georgie," she shouted down the stairs and I stuck my head in the well and shouted up to let her know I was all right.

"The halls are full of bad people," she'd said. Only people trying to escape the day. On every landing they sat. Men and women alone, together, bowed heads, smelling of themselves and cheap wines. They opened red eyes at my approach and I wondered could they see with eyes so filmed and dull. Women with skirts pushed to their hips, trying to scratch and cool the dark between their thighs, showed scabby scarred legs and torn panties. Patting their hair in place, they gave me guilty gummy smiles. They didn't frighten me, they were as much a part of the building as the creaking stairs, swaying banisters and dumbwaiter squeaking between floors. Pieces of living statuary, friendly and familiar placed along the stairs like channel lights to guide me. What harm were they, they gave me a security in dim forty-watt lit halls, but how had they come to be that way, still as rocks and trees yet retaining the form of man?

Sun and I stand waiting, hear her wheezing and plodding up the stairs, she's a big Aunt Jemima woman.

"I don't dig this shit, copping in hallways. This is how a sucker gets taken off. Those sick junkies hanging round down there laying for a lame copping dope. You got a knife on you Georgie?"

"No."

"I ain't got my shit with me either, we'd really be uptight if . . ."

The arrival of the big woman interrupts him. She hands him the two packets and takes the money.

"How's the stuff?" Sun asks her.

"Dyno. Dig Sun, you and your man be cool going down."

"Why baby?"

"Broadway's downstairs with Boy and Sugar. Think they're laying for you."

Remember the sawed-off shotgun in Broadway's belt. Boy and Sugar are legendary, kings of the takeoff artists.

"I'll catch you later Sun," and she starts downstairs.

"Look Georgie. You take the dope and wait here, I'll go down and decoy them. Wait about ten minutes, then come down. I'll meet you at the house."

I sit on the stairs, putting the stuff in my shoe, listening to him go down. I'm not surprised at what's happening and having anticipated the encounter am calm. Wait for what seems ten minutes, then start down when I hear someone run in the building. Looking down the well, see three hands coming up the banister. It's too late to hide. Start upstairs quietly. They come noisily behind, stopping on each floor to search the shadows. Hear disturbed junkies and winos protesting. Reaching the roof, push through the door and stand a moment listening. They've heard the door and are running. I take off toward Madison Avenue, bounding across the four-foot spaces between buildings six stories in the air. Looking back, see Broadway point me out to Boy and Sugar. They continue after me while he runs down into the street to cut me off. Coming to the corner house, run in and dash downstairs. Reaching the ground floor, peer cautiously out. Broadway is patrolling the street looking up at the roofs. Going to the back of the hall, I try the door to the backyard, it's locked and Boy and Sugar are coming down the stairs. Can hear them talking, "Kill that motherfucker," and suddenly I'm afraid. Fear, the sudden realization that your life can be taken, that it can be taken and you aren't ready to die. This is the only fear and standing there I realize that these fools can kill me and no one will care. When they stretch me out and see the monkey marks on my arm it will go no further, just another dead junky good riddance.

Hunted. I tense like an animal, am keen, the hair on my body raises on end. Gathering myself I burst from the building running to Madison. Spotting me Broadway shouts, "Georgie wait a minute!" Boy and Sugar come from the building shouting, "Catch that motherfucker!" I fright and take off.

Sprint downtown, hoping to lose them in the crowds on 116th Street. *La Marketa* is jammed with shoppers, but it doesn't hinder the chase. Panic speeds me and over my shoulder I see them pushing through and getting closer. The avenue becomes a bizarre tropical forest. Cars are wild unmanageable beasts prowling and blocking the streets, coughing and barking noxious breath into the air. Sun-softened tar sucks at my soles like quicksand. People block and snatch at me like serpents or vines. Break free of the crowds and race madly ahead, afraid to turn left or right into a side street with few people where they can have their way with me.

112th Street. Have run five blocks and am dying. Chest burning and legs turning rubber. A cop walks onto the avenue and I slow, thinking here is help. I'm being robbed, but he cannot help me. I'm being robbed of dope, contraband, fair game for all. Am not of his world or protected by his law. Beyond the pale. Once

past him we begin the chase again. I spot a cab and dodging traffic, jump in. Lock the doors and start to roll the windows up.
"Downtown, Sixty-sixth and Columbus."

Broadway rushes up, knife in hand and forces the window
down. I punch and kick at him but still he hangs on. The old Jew
behind the wheel frights and floors the gas dragging him half a
block till he falls sprawling to the street. Sitting on the ground
holding his knees, a grin splits Broadway's face and he waves.

"What was that all about?"

"Nothing." I fall back into the seat. It would do no good to tell
him what happened, he can't understand. It happened in another
country, a place where his concepts and values have no meaning.

Turning downtown at 110th Street onto Central Park West,
relief washes over me. The energy that possessed and sustained
me leaves, am free, no longer prey to the menacing mood of the
jungle or marauding Broadway. The black brick wall bordering
the park at 110th Street is only three feet high, but unscalable and
impenetrable as any wall closing off a prison guarded by towers
and guns. I'm safe beyond it. Broadway cannot chase here. He has
lived behind the wall all his life and is imbued with its lifeway,
which so contradicts this world, that here he is rendered impotent
and unable to function. Consider that he goes days without seeing
a white face, and living in the street is not influenced by TV and
newspapers, so is not even reminded of them in that way. That
he knows whites only in positions of menacing life-and-death authority, policemen, judges, and prison screws. That he hates and
fears them.

He would not pass the wall and enter this place, confusing and
uncomfortable. If he were to, he would vanish, he and all those
despairing blacks, because in this world they do not exist.

II

LEAVING THE CAB AT LINCOLN CENTER, descend into the arcade connecting avenues, avoiding the crowds around the splashing fountains and outdoor eating area. Hate walking through the Center, its massive buildings, institutional and temple-like, their formality, all whiteness and glass.

Halfway through the arcade it begins. From the tunnel's mouth, a racket so loud, as of huge insects buzzing and as you get close, you identify the sound of people, spics and niggers, talking loud, screaming and shouting over the roar of traffic and commerce. An ice cream man's bell clangs. Exiting, you are plunged in uproar, your eyes are tortured up to the gaping raw façade of a housing project stretching four blocks long and thirteen stories into the air. It is the casbah, the quarter, the hum of hawkers at bazaar and breeze blown curtains flapping madly from windows. There is something exotic about this dislocated piece of Harlem, the teeming crowd that trundles ceaselessly about the towers. They're everywhere, hanging from windows, cars, mailboxes, each other, anything that will support their weight. The men posed before the bar, hands in pockets, or leaning on a fence, watching the young girls and women cart kids and groceries past. Everywhere the kids, hundreds of them, running and milling about like beasties under glass, yelling out their favorite obscenities, vicious and tough.

Hurrying across the street, I enter the project, greeting acquaintances. I lived here for years and know most of the five thousand residents. Every few feet I'm stopped by someone asking the health and fortunes of myself and family. From windows and doorways come shouted hellos. The ritual of greeting carried out when meeting on the street, I perform ten to twenty times before I get where I'm going. Once this filled me with self-importance, being hailed and saluted by so many. That so many recognized and knew me. I was a hero, raised and adored, set above by them. I was going to make it for them and get out of this stinking pocket of existence. They knew Georgie Cain, All-American basketball player and student. They told their children, "Be like him, not like me."

And I failed them, falling back into the pit they so wanted me to escape, for their sake, my sake, just to see it done. Even now, few know or would believe where I've been these last years. They only know that I've failed, not caring how or why, only that I've failed and because of it am somehow more like and closer to them. Their acknowledgment is pleasant and necessary now, giving me a sense of being in a world constantly negating my existence.

Passing the playground, I see kids running ball. It's unchanged since I played. Benches crowded with onlookers, old men, young men, girls and women. The old men serve witness and testify to the generations of neighborhood ballplayers they've seen and compare them with those out there now. The young men recall themselves a few years ago and the young girls and women love the dripping black bodies running in the sun.

They play more than a game here, for this is the battleground where so many heroes die unknown. Whites amuse themselves by asking who was the greatest performer in a sport, they quote figures, statistics, give college and professional records and show you a picture. Ask me the same question and I say Bootsy was the best. Who is Bootsy? What school did he go to? I don't know. I don't even know his name and he didn't go to school, but you can find him nodding on the corner of 116th Street and Lenox.

Nowhere except in play can blacks compete fairly, for unlike life the rules of the game are indiscriminate. The spectators know this and esteem their athletes raising them high above. I played harder in this playground before fifty people than in Madison Square Garden before twenty thousand.

Pop, an old man, self-appointed referee and scorekeeper waves and calls me over. It's between halves, the players are resting and those not good enough to play toss shots waiting for the action to resume.

"Still got your eye?" Pop calls out. "That corner used to be your spot. How you been Georgie? Still playing ball?"

"No Pop not anymore."

"What? Always expected you to make the pros, you could really play. But maybe it's best. You remember what I use to tell you about the pros? They're crooked. It ain't like out here, the best man can't always be the best. Gamblers run the pros. It's a fix. They tell a man they want a close game tonight, so cool it, don't score so many. That's how it goes down and if a cat wants to play, he got to go along with the program, where else is he going to play?"

"Game time!" somebody shouts out.

"I got to call the game Georgie, catch you later." He saunters onto the court, a tired old man knowing the whole world's a fix, and the best never is.

The playground is the promenade of the area, where people

gossip and enjoy the sun. Sitting in groups they discuss their own and the world's situation. Young mothers with newborn occupy the sunniest spots, talking girl talk and dreaming of marriage. Their youth and the radiance of life-giving are still in them and they're proud of their offspring. They've been told but cannot believe their lives are over. At sixteen while still young and pretty? Every summer, a new group of innocents grace those benches, children bearing children, innocence begetting innocence while the men laughing repeat an old adage, "Summer will show what winter has done," and try guessing the fathers of the children.

In the shade, from a litter of broken bottles, winos bother passersby. The toughs stand at the entrances, clean and pretty, talking shit and jingling chump change in their pockets. Kids run everywhere, knocking balls and riding bikes dangerously, tonight they'll make sport of snatching purses from the patrons of the art center. In a corner away from prying eyes junkies nod and dribble surrounded by shopping bags of loot they haven't sold yet. I wonder if anyone has a radio for sale.

Someone calls me from over there and unable to see that far, walk over. It is J.B. the storyteller. The storyteller found in all civilizations, preserver of unwritten histories, keeper of legends and the oral tradition. Daily he holds forth, as if in an African marketplace. Surrounded by black faces reflecting the moods of his narrations, he translates what is in the white mind and media into the idiom of his audience. Every corner has its J.B., that funny nigger who makes a crowd dance with laughter at themselves and their shortcomings. A comical conscience who tells the hurting truth so sweetly you love to hear it. It is a weekday afternoon and only the bad boys and young surround him, the rest of the world is workaday and rushing living a lie that James is revealing to his audience.

Many dismiss him as bullshit, unable to see his role or contribution, but like all poor black people, they're respectful of knowledge so don't protest him too vehemently. On weekends even the squares hang out and learn the subliminal truth, then go home and tell friends and family the incredibly funny lies they heard. All the while spreading his gospel. In the absence of truth-telling media James and those like him evolved. Street corner philosophers with all the technique and craft of gifted actors they hold the most difficult audience in the world.

The bad boys, Poly, J.J., Pigknuckle, Ray, Mo, Beefy, Snake and the rest. Approaching, I sense their hostility and childish fear raises in me. As a child, was told to stay away from them because they were bad and I came to think of them as inherently evil and able to draw one to hell merely by association. I've passed them a thousand times in the street without speaking. I didn't believe they spoke but grunted, communicating in an argot peculiar to blacks of which I then had no ken. But I was different, better than they somehow. Behind my guise of superiority, I feared them, with their tough speech, rude manner, their unpredictability and knife in pocket violence. But that was long ago.

Pleased to see me J.B. leaps from the bench.

"Hey nigger how you been. My man give me some splow."

We swap fives and laugh.

"Good to see you bro." Turning to the others. "You know Georgie don't you?"

They acknowledge neutrally withholding their acceptance, waiting to see how I show.

"This is my nigger here, me and him been through some shit together. When did you raise?"

"Couple of weeks ago."

"Been a long time. Man you look beautiful. I ain't no faggot but I just got to tell you, you're beautiful. Big, healthy, your eyes clean. Your color, you been out in the sun a long time. You're pure that's what it is, like a baby, you ain't been out here long enough to fill up on that poison. Man I can't get over it, say Pig don't he look good. You too use to yourself to see what I'm trying to tell you, but shit you're looking good, should try and stay that way. So what you doing to them out here in the big world, knocking them dead I bet. See you still fucking around."

"Ain't doing nothing."

"On parole?"

"Yeah."

"Know that's a drag."

A jug passes round and Pig offers me a taste. Once I would've refused or wiped the lip of the bottle and soiled the moment, but I know its significance, they're offering me their blood, acceptance, an opportunity to right my guilty past. I swallow greedily. Feel it fall a warm ball in the stomach, warming me. A restraint lifts from us, have made communion, taken part in a sacrament, their new knowledge of me, the prison, the drinking of wine and word nigger. I'm one of them and silently we acknowledge and accept each other. We feel brotherhood and know we are of the same blood.

"What was the name of the joint?" Pig asks.

"Texarkana."

Texarkana, a name strange sounding, exotic like so many others. Sing Sing, Coxsackie, Tehachapi, Chino, Longpoch, Tallahassee, Walla Walla, foreign names denoting foreign lands with strange people. There's a jail or prison in the smallest community, one day they'll build a wall from Beantown harbor to L.A. manned with guns and towers cause everyone will know this thing they call living ain't shit.

"I ain't never been Texas South, what's it like?"

"You been in prison Mo and they all the same."

"Yeah that ain't no lie."

We laugh and the bottle comes round again. A radio plays somewhere and a black voice screaming, souls, "Blueschild baby."

Sudden interruption, an alarmed white voice screams urgently, "Bulletin! Bulletin! We interrupt this program!"

All my life I've heard these flashes, tensing with anticipation because one day the voice will tell me that it's all over, an atomic bomb is coming. Instead, some insignificant natural disaster, flood, drought, earthquake, life will go on. Now it is the governor of New Jersey, "This isn't revolution, this is criminal insurrection." There is more but lost to the squeal of static.

"'This is criminal insurrection.' Ain't this a bitch. If the brothers don't get it together now, they ought to die. You know what the fool is saying? He's telling us what everyone of us knows but refuses to believe. In this place, we're criminals and treated like. It's like prison, every brother should go. When there, keep expecting to feel different but you don't. Know why? Cause you been in prison all your life. Once you know this, pressure is taken off your brain and you can think, you can do anything cause you got nothing to lose." J.B. becomes a preacher leading a congregation. "Say it to yourself. Yes, I'm a criminal and I'm free."

"Ain't that a bitch. Criminals." Pig laughs.

Listening to them I know what it is, caught in the wine and fervor I say it to myself, "I'm a criminal." Feel it build and burst in me. I'm free. Free from illusion, with license and will to think and act without the lies saying you're free. In prison you know you aren't, the reality of bars and walls proves it. But we're free now from the lie that has stayed our hands so long. No less a person than a governor has told us, how can we not believe and not act accordingly? No longer bound now by law we knew wrong but respected, fearing consequences, and all along we'd been suffering the consequences and had yet to commit the crime.

"You know they got the Army National Guard and everybody else out there shooting brothers like horseshit? Tanks, machine guns. Can you imagine a tank coming down Sixty-fourth Street spitting fire and rumbling through the playground?"

Someone snickers, most of us are young and have never seen war except in book and film and the image is beyond us.

"That shit sounds unreal, but that's what they doing. The man ain't jiving, he's looking to take us off the planet. We done got dangerous talking that shit about we going to burn baby burn, only thing going to burn is us till we get it together and stop snatching shit out of stores and start taking heads."

A young boy rushes to defend the riot and his peer group, for they are the major participants. "Yeah but this is the first time we ever really got down."

J.B. looks at him, mock incredulous, eyeballs bugging out his head as if he cannot believe such stupidity. "Say what? First time we ever got down. Nigger is you crazy? We been rumbling this man ever since we showed. You think we laid down and played dead for this shit? Thought you had better sense than that, but shit it ain't your fault, you went to one of those good white man's schools and got a good white man's education. You oughta know they ain't never told the truth about nothing, especially about you. You think they want to roil all you crazy niggers up by telling you your fathers, grandfathers, and their fathers fought every way they knew how. No good. Only brothers they going to tell you about is those good jeffin niggers.

"You think you raising hell now, let me tell you bout in 'forty-three. You ever hear of the zoot suit riot? Go ahead, laugh motherfuckers laugh, that's right the zoot suit riot. Know it ain't in none of them textbooks and they try and act like it didn't happen, but I was there and know what went down.

"Was in the Marines, Camp Pendleton, San Diego and all

they had were these cracker, motherfucken sergeants. They was a bitch. They were so fucked up they couldn't say Negro, they'd say nigra and make it sound so nasty and fucked up and used to hate us brothers from the North.

"'Ya'll is a Yankee nigger ain't ya'll boy?'"

We broke up at his mimicry, twisting his face and mouth as the sergeant must've done. Posing with hands on hips.

"I looked at this big hat-wearing cracker motherfucker and said, 'Ya'll, who the fuck is he, I don't know no ya'll, my name's James Black.'

"'Boy I see ya'll one of them smartass Yankee niggers, ain't ya boy?'

"They didn't like you talking to em smart, but they was afraid of a nigger from a big city, they thought niggers and gangsters ran New York and Chicago. Our outfit didn't have nothing but brothers in it, and man we gave our C.O. so much static he went crazy and got a transfer and they sent a Yankee down.

"Had this partner of mine Ace, outta Chicago, me and him won all this bread gambling and bought a brand new Lincoln, color hot pink. Had it done up special. We go on up to Frisco and snatch off a couple of them blond-haired blue-eyed bitches and bring em on down to Tijuana. Be partying and shit, making the clubs and sure enough we'd run into one of them jiveass sergeants. They hated to see us with one of their women.

"'Black, what ya'll doing with them white women?'

"You heard them talk? I'd been around em so long, got so I could imitate em good as I wanted to. We use to call it crackio, the way they talked and they hated when I went into my act. Knew I was fucken with em. Anyway I say to this sergeant, and dig I got my hand all on the bitch's ass and shit, 'Sarge, what ya'll think I'm gonna do with this here fine blond-haired white woman?'

"And the hole, she be goofing this sucker too, laughing and pulling on my dick. Man you should've seen him burn, he turned deep purple and started strangling on himself.

"'Black, ya'll know when ya'll get back to base, your ass is mine.'

"Come out my butch bag then.

"'You don't stop fucking with me and your ass is going to be mine right now Sarge.'

"By this time the word done got round and all the sergeants are on my ass, but I don't give a fuck, going to do what I'm going to do anyway. I come into the barracks one day and this sergeant says, 'Black what'd you do them pants?'

"I was so slick, had all my uniform pants pegged. This lame takes my pants and calls the entire company out on field, he got my pants holding em up so everybody could see and says, 'Look at these here britches.' I'm standing there next to him clean as the Board of Health. 'This is how Private Black gallivants about town.'

"Ain't that a bitch, he calls my pegs britches, you know how that killed them crackers, man they fell out, the whole fucken company. Felt like breaking my leg in the fool's ass. Sucker threatened to court-martial me for destroying government property, but that didn't stop nothing. I'd leave camp with em under my arm and the minute I was outside the gate I'd put em on. Old Sarge'd come by.

"'Black, I done told you about destroying government property.'

"Tell him to kiss my ass then and kept getting up, was off base then.

"Remember when all the brothers got together, we'd be talking a hip and slick shit, a roony ofay and whatnot. This old redneck'd come and ask what we'd be talking bout. I'd fuck with em, they'd get mad when you wouldn't tell what you were talking about.

"'Why you want to know Sarge?'

"'So I can understand ya'll.'

"'You don't ask them Mexicans or Filipinos what they're saying.'

"'Well they's different Black, they's foreigners, we Americans. They talking another language, you and me we both talking English and we got to understand each other.'

"I'd tell them fools anything."

"What about the riot J.B.?"

"Say man this is my story, I'm coming to the riot. The shit kicked off in this bar downtown San Diego. Generally the brothers went to this one Mexican bar, but this night four or five of these cracker sergeants were there and one of them started fucken with this little Mexican. Next thing I know this sucker pulls a machete out his ass and cuts the sergeant's throat. Blood flew everywhere, should've seen those crackers haul ass. This one cat, his head was hanging on by a piece of skin, eyeballs rolling round and blood just bubbling out his neck. You ain't never heard no shit like this. Ever hear a cleaver go through meat and bone and smack that chopping block? That's how it sounded, whomp. After that the shit started, them crackers came back with more crackers looking to do something and we rumbled, all the niggers and pachucos rumbled those devils. They called out the Guard and we split to Mexico, was AWOL for ninety days. Swear on my mother, may God strike her dead if I didn't kill me a devil. That's right, I brought one of them fools out his life. That was in 'forty-three. You didn't know about that and a lot of suckers got wasted. They tried to hush it up and say it didn't happen, but I was there and know better. Think how many other things we don't know about, that they ain't telling."

We stand about commenting and I feel sick. An ache in all my bones, chills, the junk leaving in a sweat from every pore.

"James you got any works?"

"I don't fuck around anymore Georgie but I got some stashed on the roof."

Making farewells, we leave the group and hurry through the project. Everybody and thing here is a warm memory of a time when all was new impressing indelibly on consciousness. Growing old was only a loss of innocence and now everything is bound in habit. Life with no consciousness of life, meeting experience with a stock of pat reactions, nothing is new, initiated or willed. I'm dying and need a shot of dope.

WE ENTER THE BUILDING and the past closes on me. I lived in this building for years. Everything is unchanged, like an exhibit in a museum, a period piece of another time and place. Hear the elevator moving, stopping, starting and finally opening on us. It is the same, the ever-present puddle and stink of child's pee in the center which forces us to the corners of the car. Starting up and apprehension, a fear from childhood.

A child was unable to reach the desired buttons save one, a pretty white-lettered red button. The car stuttered up, alarm sounding urgently. Closing doors and movement frightened him and he'd scream for his mother. Then it would stop as if at his fear and open on a hall exactly like his, white brick façade and five steel blue doors in corresponding positions. He knocked on the one thought his and strange faces appeared, hostile voices. Insane questions. "Who are you? What do you want? You don't live here, go away." And the door would slam. He'd stand crying, not knowing where to go, where was his house, father, mother, above, below, maybe they were gone and he'd never find them. Maybe they never were and his life had been a dream. To try the stairs was folly, a thirteen-story stairwell was a universe in vastness from which he might never be rescued. He'd reenter the car and his mother hearing his cries would press the button and bring him to her, hug him and ask what was wrong. It was beyond his ken how she rescued him each day from the losing vastness and he thought it magic.

The elevator shakes to a halt. Remain silent, not wanting to say anything stupid or reveal where I've been. So vivid memory. To make me think to speak would be to do so in child's voice and to be seen, in child's aspect.

Exiting, we creep softly to the upper landing. While J.B. watches the stairs for police, I cook up. Junk stench hits my nose and I taste the wine rising in my throat and am wracked with dry heaves. Finally, I fix myself.

Sit nodding, distant and far away I hear J.B. "I got to pray Cain."

He pulls a prayer mat from out his pocket. His prayers sing on the air, covering me in grace and I kneel. No words leave my mouth, but something long dormant stirs at center of self and we speak as original man before the fall. His movements are strange, but one, *sadja,* prostrate and submissive I assume naturally and stay there frozen feeling myself move confidently in vastness. There is harmony within, without and the light of childhood that pervaded all moments with God floods my brain.

THE TIMELESSNESS OF SUNDAY. One knew it without calendar, it was the day of rest, when the world ceased turning and all things were held in abeyance. Troubled in mind? Sunday would come respite and Nana dressed in white to take us to church. The day always clear, and washed, ragamuffin children dressed in Sunday bursting with mischief restrained themselves for three hours while Reverend McKenzie, a shouting preacher working in frenzy chanted in a singsong. He looked down from the pulpit, intimidating, eyes dilated, head back and skinny arms flaying the air.

"Brothers and sisters this morning I want to tell you bout the Good Samaritan. You all know the parable."

He drew his brows together and fire came from his eyes and he screamed. "But do you really know what it means? No you don't. No you don't know. But I'm going to tell you. I'm going to tell you what it means to each and every one of us today. There was a man ..."

His breath comes short, voice softens as he sings the story. "Yes Lord. There was a man. Hurt. Laying by the roadside. People passing saw him ... his pain and misery and they did not stop. Why didn't they stop?"

He screams. "They did not stop. They're you and me, so occupied with ourselves we cannot stop. Cannot stop to help our brother in his pain and misery."

And he sings softly. "But there comes one. Yes Lord. There comes a man. A man of God." Pauses to gather his strength. Pulpit-pacing and sweating. Wipes his face with a silken rag.

All about the agonized sinners cry, "Oh Lord. Alleleujah. Amen. Yes Jesus. Thank you Jesus."

In them there is pain, shame. They are those people passing their hurt brother. A thought races through the congregation and unable to be contained bursts out, "Help me Jesus! Oh Lord!"

Once loosed you feel so good, all evil is expelled by your cry to God. Confessing publicly before the entire world.

And the preacher sang soothingly to reassure them. "Yes brothers. There came one. A man of God who saw his brother's pain and stopped to help him."

Now shouting. So tired. "Yes Lord. He stopped. And he helped him. He took him home. He cleansed him. He fed him. He clothed him. Oh Lord. He helped this man."

The congregation groaned and cried at this goodness and speaking softly he told it all. "He helped him not for gain." Shouting—"He helped him cause he had God in his heart. Yes, he had God in his heart. Why don't you give him a chance. Yes give him a chance. When you see your brother's misery all about you. Don't turn away. How can you turn from your brother. Let him into your heart. Extend a helping hand. Yes Lord let God come into you. Amen brothers. Amen."

Grace flowed all round you then, warm and golden, you were that Samaritan, helping your brother whom all others had forsaken. God had answered and was in you. Chords from an organ sounded warm and golden. Vacant eyes and ecstasy all about. Then song. The young voice chorusing with others made joyful noises unto God. In that instant believed myself an integral part of the community of man. All men, past, present and future were related, brothers. Tasted eternity and as I began to grasp the secret of this unity it vanished, leaving elation at the glimpsed beatific. Nana said it was impossible for man to grasp in his imperfect state, but given brief glimpses to reveal what is the Kingdom of God. We sang and our love covered us. We were in one another, all emanating love, growing strong and beautiful from one another. Kept time clapping and happy sounds raced through the small building, spilling onto the street. Passersby stopped and listened. Drawn they peered in and bathed in love were unable to leave and what had been so important moments ago and sent them hurrying down the street was relegated to time and place and unto God what is God's.

FINISHED WE GET OFF OUR KNEES and lean over the parapet. Up here the madness of the streets seems distant. It's turning evening and the sun falls into Jersey. Peace leaves me and the world calls.

"Come on James, let's make it."

We stumble from the roof into the elevator and start down. I press all the buttons and at each landing pull James from the car. "They're all the same. See all the same."

On the third floor, we hear the grumbling of people downstairs in the lobby waiting for the elevator and leave to walk down. Air hits me stirring the junk inside and I feel faint, am suffering narcotic poisoning, must get somewhere before I go out.

"You okay Cain?"

"Too much dope."

"Come. I'll walk you."

We head toward West End Avenue to avoid eyes and hide my shame. Away from the project we change. Our voices and gait tighten, we've entered into the other world and its white inhabitants flowing around us like water round rocks make us uneasy. James's eyes flash from one white face to another trying to read their eyes while they pass uncomfortable.

"Dig it Cain. The man is mad. Look into his eyes, see how afraid he is. He's afraid. Afraid of everything, afraid of getting mugged, afraid for his property, afraid of niggers, afraid of Russia, afraid of China and most of all afraid of dying. Ain't that a bitch, afraid of what's got to happen. Fear is what's driving him mad. The other day I was reading about some guy who burned. He had so many locks on his doors and windows, he couldn't get out the house. Tell me that ain't some crazy shit. I can't live like that, let fear lock me behind a door. Make me stay in the house, own so much shit I'm afraid to leave cause someone will take it. What the fuck happens out there Cain, what's with them people, what do they do to you?"

He asks the question sincerely, like one would ask an astronaut who'd been to another planet, "What's it like out there?"

A white woman passes, I smell the sex and lust on her, she eyes us. Watching James out the corner of my eye, he dogs her and turns away guiltily. "Can't help myself, got a thing for those white women."

She has seen his glance and is satisfied, seen the lust in his eyes. They play for and expect it from every brother they see. But that is all they'll see, lust for the fragile white flesh they tease us with. There can be no love for them, their souls or minds, only the lust conditioned into us. But some have overcome conditioning through intimacy with them and no longer pleasure them with their glance. It disturbs and intrigues them when one does not respond to the bait. These are the dangerous ones who have tasted of the Man's most prized possession and found it bitter and lacking. She has stopped now and flaunts her body. It has become a contest of wills, but I will not be tempted.

"Say man that broad is giving you big rhythm. Want me to split?"

She has started something in me and I feel threatened, out of place. "Come on. Let's make it uptown."

We walk over to Broadway and go down into the hole. The platform is crowded with workaday people, huddled up in newspapers avoiding each other's eyes. Here the madness is obvious. Everything contributes to it. The noise, the heat, the crowds pulsing and flowing like an animal. We are pushed into a car full of smelling, balky cattle and scream off through the tunnel. The Man cannot stand the cities, the noise drives him mad, silence is his heritage. The caves of Caucasoid Europe were quiet, desolate. But we are of tropic jungles where the noise level is intense. Cats scream and insects call. We can handle the sound and shall own the cities one day. We shall not have to kill the Man off. He will do it himself, his system has a built-in suicide mechanism. They talk of nuclear holocaust and we shall all die, but it ain't so. Only the guilty shall. Contracts are made with Allah and man must stay the duration. He cannot renege.

Flashing through the 86th Street station, I decide to take the junk back to Sun. A typical high junky gesture. Once high you are overcome with generosity, as if in attempt to atone for all the wrong you've done. We are pushed out into a steaming, teeming Harlem night of red neon and shifting crowds, heavy odor of fish and chips, nausea. Everywhere there comes music with lots of bass and the buildings blurred by neon are a strange landscape of dark boxes falling down. But there is a warmth, that love bond. It is the jungle, that is what they say, but it's warm, it made and protected you. Darktown comes to life in the dark. Night is its natural garb, making soft its harsh lines and mounds of litter. Brothers on the street acknowledge James's tarbush, the brimless hat of the Muslims, with Arabic greetings.

"*A salaam aleikum,* brother."

"*Aleikum salaam.*"

"Peace brothers."

"Say James, let's go to the Playhouse want to dig some sounds."

I walk without the tension of downtown and recall how I once feared this place. Harlem was some hell escaped, into which I never wanted to fall again. And like some dark beast or fear, it lay waiting for the slightest weakness to devour and draw me home.

We walk up '17th Street to Seventh. I lived here for a while as a child. The laundry, Democratic Club, West Indian grocery and funeral parlor. Try to recall names, Ray Ray is the only one and no image appears, it was too long ago. Looking up the block, there is a gap in the wall. I wonder has that property been vacant all these years?

This is where the fire came and took my great-grandmother. It started in the basement and came roaring up the air shaft. Clouds of smoke and you could hear flames eating closer. My Nana led us over the roof and downstairs through 1361, another building and we stood in the street hypnotized by the flames devouring our place. It was then we remembered Granny.

Her room full of things old and dead, the heavy armchair where Reverend Banks sat when he came to visit, calling her Sister and telling her, like you tell a child, of heaven with golden streets and beautiful people. Their talk of people and incidents long done. My child's mind re-created them, giving a beauty they did not possess, but couldn't be refuted since they were dead and done with. They would pray The Lord's Prayer, "Our Father Who art in heaven . . . ," his voice coming strong and clear through the curtain, hers unheard by the ear, but felt more strongly by some part of self. There was the bureau fronting the window, so high I'd never seen its top, blocking the little light coming in, dark, made of mahogany with brass handles, containing her nightgowns and toilet things, the bottom drawers were filled with my father's old playthings, a massive ball of aluminum saved during the depression, foil darkened from dust and being kept in dark, a broken spade and child's pail, locks of hair—my father's, aunt's, their old report cards, and papers recording transactions, all with Nana's clumsy signature. Remember her pulling them out and showing them to me. There was a cedar chest full of picture albums by the wall, sometimes I'd sit on it and watch Granny, the gentle rise and fall of her body caused by passing breath.

A hall ran the length of the apartment, the only rooms having doors, the bathroom to the side of the foyer and the front room facing the street. The rest were separated only by curtains or screens, and going from one to the other was like passing through different worlds, each having the scent and personality of its owner. Pushing aside the curtain, I'd walk quickly, trying to be quiet and avoid the creaking boards. A dark room softened by light through a curtain. She lay under the comforter, head propped on a pillow, features hidden by dark, but indelibly impressed upon my mind, gray hair spread over white pillow, the millions of wrinkles hiding her mouth and nose, two blind eyes, one nothing but eyelids wrinkled on themselves and sunken, the other opening on yellow iris. In the dark could swear something of vision remained to this one eye for it captured the little light in the room and shone. Under a heavy quilt, her frail body outlined, one leg ending abruptly like some mountain chain running into ocean, diabetes had cut it off.

"That you Georgie?"

"Yes Granny."

"Come closer."

Words uttered so feebly, almost unspoken, yet I'd obey as if she had shouted. She'd raise her bony hand and I'd hold it, so thin I could feel the blood running sluggishly in her veins, the touch dry and pleasant. Telling me with a touch that she loved me, that we were blood, then replacing the warm hand in its position and resuming her corpselike posture.

The only objects in the room, archaic and cumbersome, distorted by the dark and the child's mind, were friendly familiar personages. They were situated in a circle about the bed and the most amiable dialogue was always in progress. The armchair was Reverend Banks, the bureau, Brother Lofus, the cedar chest, Sister Cunningham.

The room was a vault, mingling past and present, containing the memorabilia of the family and Granny the living past, corpselike but loved and loving its keeper. When the bureau or cedar chest was opened, the past seeped out along with musty air, strange and inexplicable, requiring interpretation, Nana's mother's, father's, relatives, colored and distorted by time. I rarely entered her room during the day or light, usually in evenings when Nana called and met me at the front. Other times I came and left through the back and this lone meeting with Granny had become sacred ritual, compelling me to be frozen and pay homage to a timeless world, with time in either direction beyond her room, till some distraction, a breeze or door slamming, more often Nana urging me to hurry, "Your father will be home in a minute," broke the spell and moved me.

Coming to the gap in the wall, I see it's not my old home that is gone, but the building next door. People sit on my old stoop and eye us as we cross over to stare at the place, none are familiar or call a memory and I wonder do any of them remember my family.

"I use to live here."

They stare but none speaks.

"Lived here years ago. Was born here. There was a fire, my great-grandmother died in it and we had to move."

Sympathy shows in their eyes.

"Do any of you remember the fire or the Cain family?"

They nod no.

CAN HEAR THE NOISE of the bar a block away. Out front big shiny cars caught in neon sparkle like jewels. Inside the heat of bodies, alcohol and music warms you. J.B. orders two juices and we sip soaking in the life around us, like two batteries recharging to give us strength to go out in the other world again.

"Use to hang here when I was doing wrong. Know Mack behind the bar and most everybody else here. Be back in a minute."

He walks over to talk with a woman who was once beautiful, now she is ravaged by the junk life. The place is called Gunsmoke by its patrons but some Irish name, legacy of another time and people is on its front. It's one of those places frequented by the bottom of the world. Outcasts and renegades driven to similar palaces, this night and every other, barring its closure or their arrest. Banded together for company, comfort and protection.

Bad doing pimps sit in a corner, they've divided man into two classes, players and tricks. I despise them, their weakness, processed heads, long nails and femininity. Calling themselves strong, supermen. How strong you got to be to take money from a woman? The first woman they played was momma. They glorify themselves and their game, giving it a romance and glamour it doesn't possess. All sparkle and shine, but base and defiling to touch.

Here are petty crooks, victims thinking they're victors. Driven body and soul, they talk furtively. Searching eyes and ears, untrusting those near them as they plan the grandest larceny of their careers. They're all hip and cool, but it's just another way of dying. Some youngsters move around, protégés of the others, hanging on to every word, being schooled in the arts of vice. They're kings for a day, pockets full of pawn tickets, begging a smoke while they tell you of the big money they've had in their time. Kings for a day who live in a car and sport fashionable wardrobes the day after a success, then return them to the pawnshops the day after and hope for another sting before the expiration date falls due.

Drunkards, junkies, heads hung in their crotch, wait for a drink or fix to send them hurtling into themselves. Whores and prostitutes stand about, posing and waiting for daddy to put foot in her ass and chase her into the night to make that money. Hidden in shadows revealed for a moment by the moving colored lights of the juke. Moving in time with the music, black music, love music of youth. They look at me with their too-much-seeing eyes and call in that language peculiar to them, silence, a silence surer than voice. That silence inviting men to share them, forbidden things.

"Joanie, this is Cain. Cain, Joanie."

"Hello baby."

Her voice is cracked, tired-toned and weeping, full with the pain of life. Immediately we recognize each other as kindred and feel guilty in the presence of the pure J.B. This is why he is here. There is nothing he can tell us, cause he knows there was nothing anyone could tell him, but by the example of his life he can show us.

"Dig Cain, Joanie, got to cut out. Catch you later."

And he is gone, vanished. With him gone there is no need for pretense, not that he doesn't know the minute he is out of sight we shall do what we shall. But his purity gives one strength to resist.

"You want to get down baby? I got works and a place to get off right around the corner."

We leave the bar and hurry down the crowded street.

"Where you know J.B. from Cain?"

"Downtown."

It's an old dilapidated luxury apartment building suffering neglect. The cluster of drunks, junkies and children crowding the stoop and halls make way to let us through.

"You'll have to excuse the place, it's a mess. You know how it is."

She leads through the door which was originally the entrance to an apartment. It's a small green room with cracked and peeling walls. The only furniture, a bed, table and chair. Newspapers and clothes are strewn about and it smells of junk and cigarettes.

"Sit down. Let me go get the things."

We cook up, fix and nod awhile.

"Excuse me while I try and get this place together. I'm not like this. Really, this ain't me but you know how tired you get when you ain't got your medicine. Just so tired, ain't got energy to do nothing."

While she cleans, I look out the window.

"Say Cain I'm going down for a minute, you mind waiting here for me? Be right back."

From the window watch her head upstreet and turn out of sight, wondering where she is going. A ceiling light throws my shadow on the ground and people noticing look up at me. Turn it off banishing the room and shadow and look out unnoticed.

Night people, revelers, cars, innocent children. Activity of the street. There goes a hurried furtive dope fiend, running sick somewhere to cop. Two drunks carousing, joyously embrace, bracing one another stagger from sight. Boy and girl flirting in hall shadowkiss and finger fuck. Someone upstairs loud playing a radio. Sam Cooke sings "A Change Gonna Come." Young wino, unhearing the music, walks in its rhythm. Hurrying yellow cabs. Junky smiling fixed now returns. Air brakes on big truck. Neon signs merge in the distance. Little kids. Why are they still out? A hungry hole, hungry trick, hunting each other walk past in opposite directions. Policeman's blue coat walks past. Thinking of wife and kids, unseeing all going on about him. Pandering pimp accosts a john trick, inquiring, "Wanna buy some pussy? Any kind of woman, white, black." Murphy men and con-men hunting marks, running games on the whole world. The hole has found the trick heading for the hotel. Police and fire sirens sound frequently. Blue coat picks up plodding feet and walks away. The city's finest. That one's a detective, plain-clothes. Something tells him off, acts like a faggot. Not flat feet, it's the hunting demeanor. Trying to make a score, catch a thief. Must be the girl's mother yelling at the boy, hits her, curses her and he runs downstreet. Detective's shakedown. Legs and arms apart, against the wall, frisk him, look through wallet. He's clean, let go. Must meet his quota, make a bust before the night is over.

Where is she? Impatient, I decide to leave. Check the stairs, they're full of people, nodding and sleeping like at Nana's or Sun's.

It's a frozen timeless world. They're dust covered like old statues. The place is a graveyard filled with ghosts and wrecks of dead black people.

A racket in the lobby grabs my ear. It's one of the women. Legs splayed, hands on hips, she telling this police, "Motherfucker get your shit hooks off me."

"Sorry lady, I'm sorry. We got a complaint."

"Complaint my ass. Who're you? Putting your hands on me."

Drawn by the noise, the dead come alive and crowd the lobby.

"What he do to you baby?"

"Low-lifed motherfucker felt my ass."

"Think you can do anything you want to cause you got a badge and gun."

The dead make angry noises and become ugly. One cop raises his eyes heavenward as if calling on his God. I see the fear and confusion in his face. The place is alien and hostile, dead creatures surround him like horrible beggars with runny sores and deformities, crowding about and putting their filthy hands out to touch him. He runs from the building to the radio car. In minutes van and police arrive. A sergeant walks in, helmeted and wearing bulletproof vest, followed by fifty like him. He sniffs the foul air, then seeing the people—"It's rotten. Fucken place smells like shit." Stands like a conquistador confronting the Indian. A new world with strange people. Pointing to someone he asks, "You live here?"

"Yeah."

"Where at?"

"Upstairs."

"Let's see your welfare card."

"I ain't got it."

"Bullshit."

Pointing to another—"You live here?"

"No."

"Well what the fuck you doing here then?"

"Visiting."

"Visiting my ass. Get the fuck on out of here."

The lucky one hurries through the mass of blue, blocking the door, glad to escape.

Walking to the stairwell, the cop looks up. His blue eyes blink at fifty odd pair of brown looking down. "God damn there's more of them, call another van. Okay men, I want you to bring down every swinging dick in the place that ain't behind a door." They come up the stairs like hunters stalking cat, preceded by beaters, the commotion of scuttling feet and slamming doors. I return to the room and lock myself in and there's an urgent banging at the door. Opening, it's Joanie, wet and breathless from running. We stand at the door listening to them go by.

"Good thing you didn't get locked out, saw you standing there. We'd be in a jam out there in the hall, I forgot my keys. People are a bitch, they come in and go through the place whenever they get ready, scooping up everybody they can. Some they catch dirty, those they don't they put something on. Last week Caroline, this chick that lives upstairs, her son come by to visit. Only sixteen years old, don't know nothing bout no dope. They flagged him in the hall and put some stuff in his pocket. Breeze her old man got busted too and he took the weight."

Walking back to the window I watch them bring the victims out. Those caught sleeping in the halls and bathrooms, too high to hear or care.

"Get away from the window, someone will see you."

"Turn the light out."

She hits the light and falls into a chair. The police pull off with their cargo and the empty streets quickly fill again. Standing about, the people discuss the latest injustice committed against them, glad it wasn't their time, but knowing they're due. Arrest and jail are common experiences. Everyone, no matter how well placed, has someone close in the jailhouse and the influence of the penal colony is manifested everywhere in the street. The revolution shall begin in the penitentiaries and spread over the country for this is where the most aware minds are. They say you're arrested for crime, narcotics, prostitution, robbery, murder, but these are not the reasons for locking you away. Awareness is your crime, for once you become aware, you cannot help reacting in a manner contrary to the system that oppresses you. Very few commit crime because they enjoy doing so. They do what they have to. So many leaders are convicts. Awareness is a crime and sanity the only insanity, they are such rare qualities these days, they go unrecognized for what they are and are seen only as deviate from the madness that is normalcy.

From the jails shall come the revolution, where the oppressed, those who were hungry and stole, dared transgress the oppressor, sit in cells doing what they never had time to do in the big world, read, think, and most important, exchange ideas with their brothers. Everyone should go to prison for there certain ideas crystallize. You know you're a man unjustly punished and nothing can ever mollify that but some blood. One goes there expecting some great change, but there is nothing till one day the realization that you been in prison all your life and there is nothing they can take from you cause they took it all already. We are revolutionaries with nothing to lose and they have made so many of us. We have no voice or power, but those ideas formed behind bars, walls and gun towers.

She sleeps, hear her even breathing. The prison comes before me. It is quiet, lovers have ceased their activity as they steal to the supposedly quiet world of sleep. It begins somewhere down tier with half heard animal whines after a while rising to an inhuman chorus, crying as they're pursued through their minds by those fears they kept at bay during waking. Would be there counting the rivets in the ceiling listening to them try and articulate pain. I listened and urged them, but they never spoke.

Feel the creeping fingers moving slowly up my leg like an insect and break sleep.

"What you doing?"

"Just me baby."

Her presence, the dark and pain of her voice thrill the body. I stroke her hair and she curls against me like a cat purring softly. I haven't touched women in two years. Feeling her flesh I fill and burst into fragments. Terrible pain tears me and I struggle protest down her throat with tongue and tumble to the floor. Fumbling with unfamiliar garments my body gone mad seeks to satisfy its need, while my mind made mad in prison manufactures a dream.

Nandy, Nichole, all the women known in life pass before my mind. Faces and bodies without name, smile and call in the dark. Awailing, howling in heat, positioned to rouse they show all. Sweat and sucking noise of rocking contorted bodies heat me to fever. Hungry mouths. Sleeping with every woman in the world, black, yellow, white, a queen, the raggediest whore in the street. All come before the indiscriminating organ. That woman with the gentlemen. Young girl holding friend's arm, grandmothers and granddaughters, women at all stages of life. You old bitch riding a subway watching me out of eye's corner. Have seen your wrinkled dusty hole stuck between loose fleshed thighs. I have had you all, virgins are not virgins.

Done, no feeling. Like breathing, a necessity. An act of joy to overcome the clumsy flesh and come nearer to spirit, now done from need and lust. Retain the faculty but have lost all else, dead to rapture, despair. She sleeps quietly on my chest, feel life moving in our bodies and I want to leave and walk the streets.

I slide out from under, the junk has taken her and she doesn't stir except a sigh. Her nature is revealed in her face, soft and loving, the mask of consciousness is gone. I kiss the hot face, gather my clothes and split. I'm on the streets again, they hold me more than any drug. The peopled asphalt is home. Like the slums of Calcutta, people live in the street. Moving from one condemned tenement to another or in winter standing the night around a fire barrel on 115th between Fifth and Madison. I walk down Lenox lost in lights feeling the night pulse in my brain.

A big money domino game is being played on a card table lit by a first floor apartment. The loud banging as they're slammed to the board. The players sit and a gallery of challengers stands waiting their turn. A pause in the game, a crucial moment as one studies his play.

"Come on, play. Do I have to call the police to get you to play. Officer, officer make this man play."

They laugh at the banter they've heard so often.

"Did I bring my partner?" He shouts exuberantly having made the correct play.

"I'll stick big hurt to a chump."

"Big six to the board."

Another game begins.

"Go ahead, wolf queen counts fifteen."

The pegs move up the board counting points, the gallery taunting and jeering each play till someone shouts, "Bogus! You played bogus!"

"Bullshit!"

"You got treys in your hand!"

"I didn't pass on no treys!"

Those who know what happened, the gallery, remain mute, their silence the thumbs-down gesture of bloodthirsty Romans, spectators of death waiting for one to pull a knife and shank the other. This is what they've really come to see, for violence is in them. This place makes violence and anger a virtue. All are angry at the injustice of life. Children when angry have fits of passion telling of their frustration. So are these people turning on themselves the anger they're afraid to vent on the oppressor. Countless blacks walking the streets have taken life over some bullshit. Like those noble Romans, the gallery waits for blood, to feel it themselves. The combatants knowing all eyes are on them feel what they've never felt before. Aloof, above the anonymity of their nothing lives and once there, on that high place, it is easy to take life, give life for the gratification of the moment. They know to hesitate and let the moment pass is sacrilege, for then neither will act and both will descend lower than they were, for the others, the blood-thirsty gallery, will have nothing more to do with them and banishment is still the most severe of punishments.

A crap game is in the next doorway. Dice rattle in a palm, clicking on the pavement, come up I don't know how. The players crouch absorbed and kids sit on ashcans for a quarter watching for the Man.

"Little Joe. My point."

"Make my point."

"Come on baby."

"Four in the door."

"Fade it, who'll fade?"

"I'm hot. Lord I'm hot."

"Rollem."

"Come on. Come on."

"Be good to me dice, babies got to eat, my woman needs, my mother is dying. Be good to me."

They click and silence, everyone waiting, they face up. Little inanimate ivories, holding the mind and will as nothing else can. Groans and squeals of delight as they win and lose. It is an activity different from dope and dominoes, but its purpose is the same—diversion. To occupy the mind in those hours between wake and sleep so it will never be free to see its situation.

A skirmish breaks out over the domino game and everyone goes to see and urge it on. Two cops on the corner stand watching also.

"Pull his heart out!"

"Kill the bastard!"

"Stick him good!"

Cries from the gallery. They close, clinch and part. Their blood leaving them as they circle for another pass. Eyes bright, expectant at sight of blood, the onlookers are infected, calling for more, hurrying them together. They meet and close, desperate movements of shiny steel slash and parry. Screaming as if hurt, the spectators urge them to greater exertions till one lies down with knife in his belly. Purple blood spurts regularly from the wound. The other moves off a few feet and falls, arm hanging strangely, blood-covered, receives the plaudits of victory, smiles wearily to all and the night, then lies down and bleeds to death.

The police come and move the crowd. "Okay. Show's over, let's move it."

They move it, discussing the faults and merits of the fighters, no one knowing what'd started it. Passing the two bodies, running, I head downtown for Sun's. Coming to the park, I assume my furtive stance and cross the border. Down Central Park West on foot.

IT IS GETTING UP TO STORM. Clouds move on the moon. Wind tears night with frenzy of frustration, doubling effort at failure. Screaming then silent, scream silence. A repeated phrase, changed only by tenor of voice. Trees stand stilled. Harbinger of

storm. Dry wind chased by calm. Long torrential rain. Earth to
runny rivulets and bog-down mud. My shadow on the ground,
ringed by shadow trees sporting insanely, lashing me. Trees rat-
tling noisy, wind-blasted. My shadow more substantial than their
faint outline, looming powerful, larger than life above all, wind,
rain, oncoming storm. Forming storm fails to rouse me. Strange
feeling of unfeeling, no sensation. To feel it in my stomach, move
in it, be blown broken breadth of the plain, dismembered parts
scattered over the world, be one with the storm. Insensible senses,
dead, burned out, overflowing and puking on themselves.

The sky breaks, rain comes down like crazy. Strip my shirt to
feel it on my skin. Washing the filth off me.

COME TO SUN'S BUILDING, the warmth and light make it
welcome. It's jammed like a bus station at a holiday. All abuzz and
milling people. The dead and many just ducking the rain. Familiar faces smile and greet. Poor John an old crapshooter who's lost
his skill and life to dope calls me over.

"Hey Cain. Hear what happened to your man?"

"Who? Sun?"

"Yeah, he and Flow got flagged this afternoon. That young
gray broad Flower be with all the time? She give em up."

"Tracy?"

"Yeah, that's her. Told Sun about fucking with them whiteys. They ain't nothing but a tip. Police see a whitey round here
knows what he's doing. Why else they in a fucked up place like
this except to buy dope. Told him about that, but you can't tell
Sun nothing. He kept saying she brought him a lot of business.
All the police got to do is follow them and they'll take them to
the connection every time. Man, niggers ain't got no sense, for a
fucken dollar they'd do anything. Think he had a thing for the

bitch anyway, wanted some of that young white pussy. She was fine. Say she made good money out there too. Sun left the bitch in his room and went uptown to cop this morning, come back and she sitting there with the police waiting for him. They say she's wrong anyway, ain't the first time she done it. They ran her from downtown so many people was looking to kill her."

Police sirens scream, coming closer and everyone freezes mid-action hoping they'll keep on past. They do and the relief affects the very building with sighs. Immediately there is a commotion to leave and nervous chattered speculation on what the police are up to. There are sirens all over the night. Sojo rushes in soaking and breathless to report that a bar has just been held up and some people shot. Knick Knack comes up to us with details.

"Ain't that a bitch. These kids is something else, two of em just stuck up the bar and when the cat didn't get up off the bread fast enough, blew him away. Those young boys don't be jiving, they mean business and the sooner these people out here realize it the quicker they'll give up that cash, bet we don't read about too many hold-up heroes for the next week or so if this makes the papers."

"Yeah, but they making it hot as a motherfucker out here."

"Damn John, you done got old. Don't understand nothing no way. You from that old school. These kids out here is fast, fast, fast. Know what they want and how to get it."

"Yeah, but they still making it hot."

"Ain't that a bitch."

Knick Knack breaks up laughing at John. "Nigger it's always been hot for me, ain't never been cool, so it ain't no big thing. You just done got old and don't know what's happening. Guess John told you what happened to Sun?"

"Shit, long as Sun been on the set, he knows the name of the game, cop and blow. He let his cunt collar overrule his reason."

The police burst in the door and everyone stampedes up the

stairs hollering and screaming like mad as if noise is somehow going to help. Poor John leads up to his top floor room and entering slams the door on us. We bang on the door.

"Get out of here, go over the roof!"

We can see and hear the police coming upstairs. Taking their time, methodical. Guns drawn, rapping on doors, busting in those where there is no answer or refusal to open, herding the tenants into the hall. Lining them against the wall while an eyewitness to the robbery looks them over.

"I'll kill that nigger when I catch him. Come on Cain."

We climb the ladder to the roof thinking to cross over and come down in another building. Pushing through the trapdoor we jump into wet night, pausing to get accustomed to the dark then running over to the next building. The hatch is locked and adjacent buildings too far away. We scramble around like rats looking for a way off. None. I remember the dope in my pocket and stash it behind a chimney. Knick stands on the edge of the roof emptying his pockets of identification into the backyard. I do the same.

The light beam picks us out.

"Move and I'll blow you off this building."

"On the roof! There's two of them up here," one shouts down to another.

"Turn around and walk over here with your hands up."

We obey, moving carefully to give them no excuse to shoot. Six cops, waiting, guns drawn, grim looking. Throw us against the chimney and shake us down. Finding nothing they turn us around and throw the light in our eyes.

"What you doing up here?"

"Man I saw ya'll coming and I got scared."

"You call me man again and I'm going to push you off this roof."

"I'm sorry officer, didn't mean no harm. I'm just scared that's all."

"I ain't done nothing. I swear afore God officer I ain't done nothing."

The others stand in the shadows, guns on us, looking down the hatch and calling to the rest to bring the eyewitness up. They're disarmed by Knick and the tension leaves the moment.

"What'd you run for if you didn't do nothing?"

"I was scared."

"What's your name?"

"Clarence Williams from Yazoo City, Mississippi."

"Didn't ask where the fuck you came from. Be still."

"I's sorry sir but I'm wet."

While he questions Knick, I think of answers. It doesn't matter what I say as long as it's not the truth. I have no papers to say otherwise.

"Where do you live at?"

"On Ninety-first Street sir."

"What you doing in this building?"

"I got some friends from home that live here, came by to see them, they wasn't in and it start raining. Was just waiting for the rain to stop."

"You. What's your name?"

"Charles Johnson."

"You live here?"

"No."

"What you doing in the building then?"

"Getting out the rain."

"What you doing on the roof?"

"Trying to get away from you."

"Why? You do something wrong?"

"No."

"That don't make no sense. What you running for if you didn't do anything wrong?"

"You know. I saw the police and tried to get away."

"Still don't make sense. You haven't done anything, but you run when you see the police."

"Ever been arrested before?"

"No."

"Bullshit. Then why you running from us? Where you live at?"

"Sixty-third Street."

"You use drugs?"

"Use to."

"Let me see your arms."

He throws the light on my arm.

"Haven't used drugs for a while I see. How'd you stop?"

"Just did."

"You should know better than to hang around a place like this. Especially since you're clean. These people, this building can't get you nothing but trouble."

The witness comes up the hatch.

"These the two stick the place up?"

"No I ain't done nothing like that," Knick whines.

"Look, I'm tired of your sniveling. Shut the fuck up."

"No that's not them."

"Look around see if you find anything else up here. Take your shoes off."

I remove them and hand them over, feeling the wet come through the socks. He inspects and hands them back.

"We can take them in for burglary. They ain't got no business on this roof."

"But I ain't done nothing," Knick whines again.

"Here's something."

One of them is messing around the chimney where the dope

is stashed. Instead of the stuff it's a spike someone else has hidden there. It's all over, we're busted. He hands it to the officer interrogating us. He looks up and smiles.

"Looks like we got you."

My mind races frantically, can't stand a bust, can't stand to go downtown. My parole, my record, my past, will convict me. Got to cop a plea. Got to talk to this man like a man.

"Look officer, why don't you give us a break. I need it. Ain't used no drugs on a year now. You can see that. Ain't been in no trouble, got a good job, my woman and kids need me. I can't go to the penitentiary for no bullshit like this. You can see I ain't using drugs."

He looks in my eyes. I look him straight in the eyes. He looks back down at the spike in his hand, wheels and pitches it off the roof.

"Get the fuck out of here and don't let me catch you on any more rooftops."

Hurry downstairs past the inquisitive-eyed dead fast as legs will carry. The police go to their car and we hustle down to the corner.

"Knick I got to make it back to the building."

"Let's go up Ninetieth Street."

As we hit the avenue, the cops pull alongside and call us to the curb. It's an old trick to discredit you on the block by being seen talking to them.

"Remember what I told you?"

"You ain't got to worry about me," Knick whines.

"Don't want to catch you again."

They pull off. We watch to see what direction they turn and go in the other.

"Niggers ain't shit. They ain't never going to be shit, cause they ain't together. Here we are being chased by the enemy, I don't mean no bullshit, but the sure enough enemy and that nigger slams the door in our face. I'm going to kill him Cain, I'm going to kill that black motherfucker. Bring him out of this life."

We return to the building and already people have assembled to argue the robbery and raid. They give us a heroes' welcome for our heroic act, escaping enemy hands after being captured.

"Here they come. Hey Cain, Knick, what happened?"

Head upstairs to get the dope, stopping to listen at John's door. I bang and yell for him to come out, know he's there.

"You better not ever come out nigger, gonna kill you when I see you!"

Go on up, retrieve the dope and kick his door once on the way down. Can hear Knick ranting downstairs about Poor John.

"Let me tell you something, a nigger ain't shit. That jive motherfucker gave us up. Slammed the door on us and told us to go on over the roof. Like there was some place to go. As long as he been living here he knows ain't no place to go on that roof. He just gave us up. Like he didn't know us or what was happening. But that's a man I done got down with, was talking to when the police came in. He knew what was happening. But it don't make no difference if he knew me or not. I'm black and so's he and when the enemy comes, you supposed to help your brother. All he had to do was let us in and wouldn't nothing have happened. As it was, we almost got busted. Had to play stuff on the Man to get cut loose. Shit, I sniveled like a baby. Lame asked my name, told him Clarence Williams from Yazoo City, Mississippi. Ain't never been out of New York in life cept one of them train rides upstate. Cain and me played it to a bust though. Shucking an jiving, scratching my head like some stupid nigger just out of big foot country. Here come Cain now. Ask him, he'll tell you what that punk ass did.

"That nigger in his room? Heard you hollering all the way down here."

"Yeah he's up there, but ain't answering."

"Well he got to come out sometime. Tell these people what he did."

"Slammed the door and told us to go over the roof. Just like that, gave us up."

"Don't give a fuck what nobody says, a nigger ain't shit. Here one of my so-called brothers gives me up, and the Man, a whitey, gives me a play. And dig, this police sure enough had us. Found a spike someone else had stashed on the roof, he could of put it on us if he had a mind. Instead, he throws it off the roof and tells us to get the fuck out of there, don't wanna see us no more. Now this is after a brother put us under the gun, so what am I to think? Ain't that a bitch, the whitey, the police. Gave us a play when our brother wouldn't. I tell you a nigger ain't shit. And that wasn't even no test. What you gonna do when it might cost your life to hide your brother? Nobody will let anybody into their house and you'll all die."

Court is in session. Poor John versus the people, charged with the crime of treason during war. A crime punishable by death. A court of his acknowledged peers shall try him. Not strangers from another country, who know nothing of him and would judge his life by a single desperate act. We are his brothers. Not that blind bitch downtown holding scales.

Guilty, guilty, L.A.M.F. is the verdict of the people. Punishment to be decided upon and administered by the offended. Today, tomorrow, for a while, John will feel the scorn of people. But one day soon, they shall welcome him as a prodigal and call him brother again. We have so much love and mercy, a necessity to maintain our humanity.

It is time for the convict to appear and accept punishment. John comes down. There is no hissing or spitting, only the condemning silence as he walks among us, beseeching forgiveness, a plea in his eyes. But there is none, anywhere. We cannot forgive, not just yet, for his shame is our shame and his weakness our own. The only place we see our oppression or what we have become is in the faces and actions of our brothers.

Daybreak is coming, pink over the buildings and the rooster downstreet calls the sun. Am hungry and have a million things to do today.

"Say Knick, I got to make it, getting late."

"Okay Cain. Be good brother."

Leaving I bump into John on the stoop.

"Dig Cain. Don't know what happened to me. Was just so sick. I'm sorry man."

I peel a bag out and lay it on him.

WALK DOWN BROADWAY heading for my room. Stop to eat in a restaurant. Place full with night people, players, and tricks tired after a busy night. I eat quickly, untasting, palate long dead to sweet and sour. Dawdle over coffee watching the people around me. Morning light is harsh and unmerciful, it shows the wrinkles and tired lines around the eyes of beautiful people so carefully covered last night. The shiny cars out front are dull with dew and exhaustion. Don't want sleep, but it steals on me, all the running is taking its toll. Pay for the meal and go to my room.

Returned to the unfamiliar place, a hole no bigger than my prison cell, a bed, window and bureau. It's a den, like an animal's, a place to hole up and lick my wounds.

Oppressive heat and wet sheets wake me. Come from sleep,

slowly, hesitant at point of waking. With closed lids listen for familiar sounds to tell me nothing has changed in absence. A habit retained from childhood when I dreamt nightmares. Always that things were changing themselves during sleep, or that I in some magical manner had been transported to a foreign place. Afraid of waking surrounded by hostile inanimate objects. Shut eyes tight till trembling, bursting open of themselves, shake my head to clear sleep. Succeed only in becoming dizzy and stumble into my clothes and out to the hall bathroom. It's in use and I knock to hurry the person inside. A woman answers, "Be out in a minute."

What time is it? No matter. Want a fix but the works are stashed below the sink. Feel a need coming on. Know I'm not hooked again, not really, it's all in my head, been there for two years. All in my head. Schemed and dreamed that first shot of dope for a long time. Couldn't get back from prison quick enough to do again what it was that got me sent away. Saw the skyline from Jersey going down into the Lincoln Tunnel and I got sick. Hadn't shot or seen dope in all that time, but I was sick, nose running, cramps, bowels tightening, nausea. The sight of Babylon brought it down on me. People thought I was crazy when I jumped down and kissed the pavement. Caught the first thing smoking to the projects. Got a fix before I saw my mother.

It's quiet. Water has stopped running and still she doesn't come out. There is a crack high on the door. Tiptoeing I look in. She stands in the mirror smiling fondly at herself, turning her head from side to side, nodding approval or disfavor at her profile. She holds a breast in the light, then the other and strokes them gently. She pats her hair and smiles vacantly at her image. Angry at her bullshitting and tying up the bathroom while the horror of detoxification is killing me. I bang loudly, impatient.

"Coming, coming."

Her voice is confused and hurried, she's just recalled herself from somewhere. Passing me she smiles the same smile she smiled at herself and disappears down the dark hall. Fix, wash and go back to the room, sit in the window planning the day. The unfamiliar room, its starkness and lack of personal articles is uncomfortable, like the nightmare. Grabbing my jacket I run into the streets.

III

I T IS EARLY SUNDAY and few people are about, pass Nellie, tired after a night on her back, we wave and go on bout our business. The winos hold down the corner, passing a bottle among themselves. I'm lost. For one wild moment don't recognize anything. The streets and buildings become strange things and I wonder where am I. Want to talk with someone, anyone, just to hear the sound of voice. Someone who is neither black nor white, whom I know so well and knows me so well we can never offend each other. Just to talk and say things that people say to one another. It's been so long, want to stop someone on the street, but only whores and faggots have license to audience whomever they want. Decide to see my mother and catch a bus at the depot. It's crowded with families going to Sunday dinner with grandparents. So long since I've been around whites, their voices and gestures are strange. Few blacks are riding my way and those that are find my appearance as strange as the whites, stealing covert glances at me, while the children stare openly. Can sense hostility everywhere. Boarding the bus, get a seat by the window and watch the others getting on wondering if anyone will sit next to me. Nobody dares. Across the aisle a white couple sit, she in a miniskirt up to the crack in her ass. She flashes for me, then looks to see if I've seen. He smiles, but I see the danger in his eyes and look out the window ignoring them.

The bus pulls out over the George Washington Bridge, the city in the hazy distance like some Gothic cathedral soars to hold up the sky its roof. We pass tollbooths and enter Jersey and immediately I feel vibrations. The whites look at me now openly hostile, while the few blacks pretend occupation. What's wrong? Passing into Jersey has released something in these people. Am afraid and wish I had a gun. This is one reason I don't visit my people like I should, they live too far away from the warmth and protection of the community. Always vulnerable, naked and defenseless out there, away from your people. We pass through Englewood and I'm the only black left on the bus.

The passengers up front hold a loud, gleeful conversation with the driver.

"That was some nigger shoot wasn't it?"

"Crazy niggers think they can do anything. But I bet they think twice next time."

"How many of them coons they kill in Newark?"

"Thirty something. God damn, for my money they coulda got every last one, save us a lot of trouble."

"I'm going out to the armory now to meet my boy. He been out there six days shooting niggers. Called me and his ma the other night. Said wasn't nothing to it, like shooting at Coney Island cept it was niggers."

Someone spots me and they stop for a moment.

"I don't care if he can hear, what's he gonna do?"

Sweat breaks on my brow and anger strangles me. Lord I wish I had a gun, want to lay hands on some white throat and feel its life struggle in my fingers. My stop comes. Walk to the front feeling

the hate and fear around me. Stepping off, I'm greeted by a fright-
ening sight, on one side of the street are thousands of whites.
Women and children waving American flags and cheering wildly.
A uniformed brass band plays "When Johnny Comes Marching
Home." On the other side rolls column after column of military
vehicles, tanks, personnel carriers, armored cars, mounted machine guns, jeeps and trucks flying rebel flags full of armed sol-
diers. My home is at the bottom of the hill and I've got to run a
gauntlet through the middle of these crazy whites.

Stunned and frightened stand wondering what to do. Get back
on the bus, but it's too late. The driver seeing my face laughs and
guns the motor pulling off, calling the crowd's attention to me.
Wish I had my shades to keep them from my eyes and thoughts. I
appeal to my reason, walk with bowed head to make sure there is
no chance to mistake my glance at one of their women, know how
they are about that. My walk is too black, too aggressive, tame
it, calm it down, become meek. Feel the pressure building in my
brain till I'm dizzy and suffocating under it. They been in Newark
six days doing what they've always wanted to do shooting blacks
and they all got guns. The highlight of their young white lives,
they'll tell it to their children like they were told about the World
War. Covered in glory and righteousness. Fuck it. Throw my head
up, get loose and stride boldly down the center feeling the hate on
all sides.

The cheering and band stop, traffic comes to a halt and they all
watch me. There are only my footfalls and the beating of my body.
I'm primed, ready like some machine over which I have no control. Waiting. Waiting for the word or gesture that will activate
the mechanism and send me to death. One will say something
and I will try to kill him on the spot. They've all got guns and I
know they will kill me, but I walk, looking them and their women
straight in the eye like I don't give a damn for none of them. All

the while ready to die. Come to a bend in the road and out of sight without incident. Hear the band and noise begin again. Sweat pours off me and I lean on a mailbox puking, two men on motorcycles ride by and shout, "Hey nigger," as they speed by. My mind races to recover itself and deactivate the machine. Returning to myself, know how a black man feels all the time. That pressure he exists under all the time till it becomes second nature, a part of him. Walking around wary of the word or gesture that will set in motion an act that will end his life and over which he has no control. Walking around ready to explode. This is what charges the air of Harlem and lets you know you're there, not the stink or sound, but the tension that lies overall like a cloud ready to burst.

Coming to our court, I check the house for any signs of unusual activity. My father sits on his throne, a lounger in the yard, surveying his domain. The big shepherd dog at his feet. He is the ruling monarch of this, his fence-defined kingdom. He waves and calls me over, I pull up a chair beside him.

"Hello George. How've you been doing?"

"Fine Pop. Doing fine."

"Working yet?"

"Not yet. Laying around getting used to the streets again."

"Good idea. But don't do it too long. You know how you get when you're doing nothing."

"Yeah."

"Your parole officer called the other day. Said he wanted to see you. There's a letter on top of the bureau for you."

"What's going on at the armory?"

"They mobilized the National Guard to go to Newark from there. Heard on the radio they were withdrawing the troops today. Didn't have any trouble did you?"

"No. Where's everybody at?"

"Your mother is inside. Keith took the twins to the city for a haircut and Sabrina. They should be back soon. Talk about haircuts, you could use one and a shave. Can't get a job looking like that."

"What'd the P.O. say?"

"Nothing much. Wanted to know if you were working and still living here. Told him I didn't know."

Sit feeling the sun cook the poison from me. Hear my mother busy in the house. Muffled and faint, the crowd and march band in the distance.

My father is old, hair turning white, gestures and manner becoming those of an old man. No longer vital and unlined. To others it is the natural process of age, but I haven't really looked at him in years and it is sudden and shocking, seeming overnight, a stranger sits beside me pretending to be my father. Calling through a window my mother saves us further embarrassment. She greets me with fierce hugs and squeezes, unlike her gentle self, trouble and stress show around her eyes.

"What's wrong Mom? Twins acting up again?"

"It's everything George. This riot, killing and whatnot, the whole world's gone crazy. Keith's become a Muslim and changed his name, running around talking bout killing and the twins they just stay in trouble, every time I hear a siren go by, I get sick."

"Nobody bothers you?"

"It's just the way they look, your father and I haven't been to work all this week. It's a good thing I shopped last week cause I can't see myself going anywhere through all them people. Getting old, can't take this excitement anymore."

They're trapped out here, at the mercy of the white mob surrounding them and showing the strain of a prolonged siege. Battle fatigue is setting in. When it comes, they will never reach the safety of the city. They'll be lynched by the white mob.

"Those twins will be the death of me. Wish you'd talk to them, they won't listen to anyone else and your father's not here during the week."

Had not understood the twins when I first saw them, but now it makes sense. The snarling, aggressive, hard walking niggers they had become at age fifteen. Unlike Keith and I who grew into an urban cool. Slick, interested, looking ahead to making it right. But their fight is more real than ours, and they are so busy protecting themselves, surviving, there can be no time for anything else. This is the front where the war is hot unlike the cold of the city and it makes you different.

"Two weeks ago Mund went to a party. On his way home he stopped at the ice cream parlor up here where all the kids hang out on the corner. He got in an argument with the help and the man called the police. Next thing I know, here comes a call from the hospital saying to come down. Nobody here but me. Your father's at work and Keith's in the city with his car. A police car with sirens screaming and lights going came to pick me up, waking the whole neighborhood up. You should've seen your brother. They had him handcuffed and in restraints. He was so angry, he was raving mad. Calling the police, the doctors and nurses, a bunch of dirty white M.F.'s and bastards. I have never heard him curse in life. So much hate in a child of mine with all that Christian background. They had to give him a sedative to calm him, maybe there's something wrong, a doctor or something may help. Well anyway you should've seen him. The police came to get him in the ice cream parlor. He hit one officer and broke his jaw. Can you imagine, a son of mine fighting the police in public. I tell you George, don't know what this world is coming to. Just be so glad when my time is up. He runs away and falls, you should see his face, it's nothing but one big black and blue scab, he says they beat him and I believe it, nobody hurts themself just falling like that. . . . Can you imagine the shock all this was at

one in the morning. So now he's got to go to court. But as if that
wasn't enough Win comes along and gets suspended from school
for punching some teacher. He says the teacher slapped him, and
so he's got to go to court too. Don't know what I did to deserve
you children. We never had this trouble in the city. Children'll
be the death of me yet, look at me, I'm a nervous wreck. They got
me taking pills cause I can't sleep at night worrying about you
children. They say the sins of the parents shall be born in the
children, so I guess we're to blame somehow. You'll put me in an
early grave, then you'll be sorry. It wasn't as if you came from a
bad home or anything, you children had everything. Your father
and I worked like slaves. Don't understand it. Don't understand
anything anymore. Keith's the only one doing well and he's gone
to acting crazy lately, talking about whitey this and whitey that.
You children ain't got no complaints, he's been good to you. The
best schools, scholarships, everything. You brought trouble on
yourself George. You went out there and deliberately ruined your
life, it took a lot of effort to do what you did. You're no victim
like some people, you made things a mess, you had everything.
Your father's district supervisor now, the highest ranking Negro
in the service. His office is in Washington and when he's home on
the weekends, looking for a little peace and quiet, what's he get,
bang, bang, one thing after another. If it's not Win it's Mund, if
it's not the twins it's Keith, always something. Keith got a scholarship you know? A full one, books, tuition, room and board, everything. That was really a blessing, but he acts so crazy sometimes.
They all act just like you, you should talk some sense to them. Do
something worthwhile with that influence for a change instead
of filling their heads with all that nonsense. I heard one of your
people on television the other day, one of those so-called brothers and he called the President baby. Now that was uncalled for.
Baby. What do you want George? What do you want? Why don't

you get a shave and haircut, you got money. Ain't no reason to go around looking like that. Put on a shirt and tie sometime, won't kill you and it'll make me happy. You say your life don't mean anything to you, well try and make me happy, just once George. I'm not asking much, just clean yourself up, it won't change who you are or what you think and you won't be so obvious. Tell you son, don't know if I'm coming or going. We got to get out of this place. Couldn't wait to get out of the city, we worked years for this house. It was going to be a good place for the twins to grow up, but they've been in nothing but trouble since the day we arrived. The police know them on sight and any time something happens involving Negro children, they come question the twins. One day they pulled them and four other children out of school and took them down to the station for questioning about some robbery. All of them under fifteen years old, down in the police chief's office. No parents or legal counsel, nothing. You know how it is with most of us out here, both parents out working to pay these outrageous mortgages. We'd never have known if I hadn't been home sick and Win hadn't called. Went down there and raised the roof, bringing those children down there on the word of some delinquent white boy whose mother wouldn't even permit the chief to speak to her on the telephone while we were there. Seems he'd been chased by some children from the neighborhood with a gun. Turns out it was pitch black when the incident took place and he was so busy running, he couldn't see anything. Well do you know what this pompous fool of a police chief says. He must've thought I was crazy, stupid or something. Well I let him know differently and just what did he think he was doing with these children, pulling them out of school and not bothering to call the parents. You know what he said? That he was trying to prevent racial incidents. Could've strangled that whitey. Oh Lord there I go talking about whitey, listening to that crazy Keith. He was trying to prevent racial incidents. How? By harassing our children who should be in school? Then he says I'm a hot irresponsible person, precisely the type of person that provokes incidents by reading prejudice into them. Could've killed him I tell you. Well I took those kids to their homes, called their parents to let them know what's happened. You know what they said. Thanks, but we work and don't have time to go down and protest. Why don't we just drop it before it hits the paper. One day this place is going to just bust apart and I don't want to be here. We're looking to sell the house and move back to the city. It was a mistake moving to Teaneck."

I know the effort it cost my mother to come to this conclusion, to sell this house and return to the jungle. It was her dream where the youngest sons would grow and escape the fate of the elder, a victim of urbanity. Years of labor and self-sacrifice. To end up surrounded, hounded and harassed by the white mob. Driven from her dream. I would kill them all if I knew how.

"What did we do wrong George? I mean there must've been something. We made all you nuts. You didn't just happen."

My father comes in and turns on the news. Hearing the sound of small arms fire I think it's a report from Nam, till I see the black civilians running through city streets. Tanks moving in such a setting is unbelievable and I keep thinking it is a movie. There's a young boy shot as a looter lying among a heap of goods. Suddenly angry my father snaps the set off. We sit stunned and I see the picture of the boy fading on the screen or is it still before my mind?

"I got something for you son."

I react to the word *son*. He never calls me son except to lecture me, to define our positions prior to talking. He is the father and I his son who must accept what he says regardless of how I feel about it.

"Come in the room, I want to talk with you."

We go inside and I sit at the foot of the bed as I always have.

Wishing I was his child son again, careless and without the responsibility for my life. Wanting to cry and have him console me, but that time is past. He fumbles about in the bureau and pulls out a wooden case.

"I've got a present for you, go ahead open it."

It's a gun, a brand new luger.

"You know how to use it?"

He breaks it down and spends half an hour showing me how to use and maintain it.

"I got that for you during the war. I've had it for twenty-five years. Kept it in good shape, knowing but hoping I wouldn't have to give it to you. Know it seems inconsistent with my position and way of life to hand you a gun, but part of a father's job is to equip his children to get along in the world. This is the last thing I can or will give you George. Everything else, a good home, education, things, all those you rejected and poisoned. Unlike your mother I don't feel guilty about anything, that your shortcomings and troubles are somehow the result of my or our negligence. She blames herself for everything, but that's a woman's way. Those things were all meant to aid you in life and this is the last thing I can give. Please, don't misuse it as you have everything else. You can leave it here till you're ready to leave. Keith went over to pick up your daughter, really you should see her. Your mother's been under quite a strain, the kids will drive her crazy."

He leaves me and I sit considering the man just revealed me. My father, a hardworking man who in all his life never hinted at anger, wanting only the best out of life and going quietly about it, advising his children to do the same. But the anger is in all of us, needing only the time or incident to blossom. Fear has done what countless leaders couldn't, rallied us together. Like a riot in the penitentiary, there is no middle ground or neutrals, color of skin determines the side you're on. No longer is there choice or free will. We're trapped in this house. I close the case and return it to the drawer.

Keith bursts through the door chased by the twins, they wrestle to the floor, laughing and bumping around. Tasha sets up a howl at her master's arrival and my mother yells for them to cut out the noise. The uproar unsettles me and I hide in the bathroom to calm myself with a fix. Hear my mother telling them I'm here and they pound upstairs to my room looking for me. I come up and they're seated on the bed.

"Hey brer," Keith greets me.

"What's happening?"

The twins rush up and we swap fives.

"Say Akbar, Abdul, why don't you two go downstairs for a while. Let me talk to George. We'll be down in a minute."

"You coming right down? Want to play you some pool for money."

"Get on, we'll be down. You two ain't nothing. Lemonade? Go get the table ready."

"Yeah Raschid you owe us money already."

"Go on down."

They leave the room arguing with themselves who'll shoot first.

"Brought Sabrina out. She's outside with Pop."

"Wanna smoke?"

While he rolls the joints, I stand in the window watching my daughter and father. Have not seen her in four years since the day she was born and find it hard to believe she is of me. A beautiful half-breed child with golden hair playing with and loving the black man she calls Granddad. From here I can hear the tiny voice and his, deep and reassuring. He is strange, my father, had never thought him capable of such open love and warmth. I've never experienced or seen it before. He laughs and smiles happily, indulging her, answering any question, pointing out things and finally packing her on his shoulders, brings her inside. We smoke and reefer struggles with scag for my head.

"So what's happening with you Keith?"

"Raschid brother, Raschid. Keith is dead. I killed him."

"Sorry, keep forgetting. The twins Muslims too?"

"Yeah, Mom doesn't know yet. She'll hit the ceiling when she finds out, already thinks I'm crazy. When you gonna make that move? Islam is where it's at."

"Got to get myself together first before I do something as important as that."

"That's true. I got a Koran and tried to mail it to you in the joint but they sent it back. Give it to you soon as I make absolution."

"How's school?"

"Okay. At N.Y.U. now on a full scholarship. You should try getting in, with your smarts and the way they screaming for brothers. They think they're slick, they got this new program for minority groups where they're bringing three hundred brothers off the streets into the school. I don't mean people who're qualified either, just three hundred blacks. All they want to do is meet this quota, knowing the brothers aren't prepared for this academic thing and when it fails, they'll say we told you so. But they don't know. Brother we got it together. Every day we drill and help each other. It's beautiful working your people, but really you should check it out. Know you can get in."

"With my record?"

"You'd be surprised. It might be an asset. They got this thing now where they're directing their efforts toward the more intractable segment of the population. I guess, figuring if they can work their magic on them, they'll have no trouble with the rest of the population. I thought they weren't going to give me a scholarship cause I wasn't fucked up enough. Didn't come from a broken home, never been busted, only thing I had going for me was that funny Army discharge."

"Let's go down."

Walking down we meet Sabrina.

"Daddy George?"

Confusion and questions flit across her face and she begins crying. Don't know how to reassure her, we are strangers. Daddy George only an identifying sound to distinguish me from the other male adults, all those uncles Nichole has had for lovers. Strangers parading in and out of her life none giving or demanding love. Only that she be quiet and go to bed early. Daddy George, someone she has been told about but never expected to see, a chimera or good luck fairy who left quarters under the pillow but never appeared. I pick her up and she clings, feel the heart and tiny body trembling against me like a frightened animal. I've seen her twice in life and she was too young to recall either time. Since then my family has taken care of her on weekends and holidays, presenting her gifts and a family in the name of Father George. I don't think anyone expected or planned us meeting. We are unprepared for one another.

SHOOTING THE LAST OF THE DOPE, feel panic race through me. Shall soon be sick without the energy to hustle money or dope. The pain begins, only a pinpoint between the eyes. It was always there, even when a child, that slight pulsing on the brain, pushing out my eyes. It will grow to consume my mind without attention. Only dope alleviates it. In prison I never knew it. It never came and I woke every morning at peace and free.

It is times like now that I've wished for a gun. When broke and at the end of hope, my sickness coming on. Go out there and take what I need from the first thing that looks like it's got it. A gun is

good as money, money is spent and goes, but a gun is constant and
never fails to bring what you want. The true Everything Card, good
everywhere with no questions asked. I put it back and hurry into
the streets to hunt a score. Am walking down Broadway checking
cars for something worth stealing when I see Lolly struggling toward me with cameras and a trunk on his back. He calls me over.

"Hey Cain you live round here?"

"Yeah."

"Look. Do me a favor? Help me carry this trunk and stash it at
your place and I'll do something for you?"

"Okay. Damn man, what in this trunk? Heavy like a motherfucker."

"Don't know yet. It's locked. Didn't have time to fuck with
it, so threw it on my back. Sorry I did now, probably ain't worth
nothing anyway."

"You some kind of thief. Taking shit and don't even know
what it is."

"Know I should've left it. Done passed a thousand police.
They're probably saying to themselves, he couldn't have stolen
that, it got to be his. Who the hell would steal something like that
and flat foot it through the streets at this hour. Nobody. That's
how you got to be, fantastic, that's why I took it. If they just saw
me walking down the street with all these cameras, looking like I
look, they'd hurry up and stop me wanting to know where a nigger got all that shit, but they see me lugging this trunk they think
just another crazy nigger."

"Better be something in this motherfucker. Heavy as it is.
Feels like books or something."

"Probably what it is, fucken books or something. Took this
stuff from a faggot's pad. He go to school downtown somewhere
and his place is full of books. Drop that shit Cain, don't need it. I
got a pocket full of dope and money."

"We're almost there. Sounds like a nice sting you made."

"Chump had about two hundred dollars' cash laying round and these some good cameras, know they worth a taste. Wish you'd been with me, could've gotten more, he had TV, stereo and things but I couldn't take it by myself without a car. This trunk was the only thing I could carry and it's too much, good thing I ran into you, couldn't carry it much further.

"Talk about luck, wasn't even out looking. Like I say, got a pocket full of dope. Don't be stealing when I'm together. Hooked on dope, not like some cats who hooked on the hassle. Stealing, just to be stealing. No, that ain't me. Was sitting up in this bar downtown waiting for Sleepy to show, when this cat slides up to me. Right away I see he's a faggot, no big thing. We get to rapping and shit and he invites me on up his house. We drink awhile and the lame hits to cop my joint and while he's on his knees, I off him. He's still out. Bet he be a mad, mad motherfucker when he gets it together."

"Here, this is it. Damn this thing is heavy."

We haul it upstairs and into my room and fall on the bed to recuperate.

"You got works Cain?"

"Yeah, let me go get em."

When I returned he's bent over the trunk.

"Still can't get this thing open."

"Want a hammer?"

"No this a good trunk here. Can get some bread for it. Don't wanna fuck it up. Might even keep it myself."

"How you gonna open it without messing it up?"

"Sleepy'll take care of it. He's good with locks and things. You got the gimmicks? Let me go first, all that work made me sick."

We get high, sit back and nod.

"Say Cain you remember when we got busted stealing them

cookies in the third grade? I'll never forget that. What was that teacher's name?"

"Mrs. Browdy?"

"Yeah, that's her, Mrs. Browdy. I'll never forget that bitch. I got the blame for it all and it was your idea. She came in the room and there I was on your shoulders reaching into her locker to get them cookies. You were so good, they wouldn't believe you could do wrong, even after you told them you did it. She made my people pay for the cookies and my mother beat me, right there in front of the class. I wanted to kill you. What'd she tell your mother? 'Mrs. Cain, you keep George away from Charles, he's no good and can't teach your son anything but wrong. George is a darling child and Charles is nothing but trouble, a bad influence.'"

"You remember that?"

"Man how could I forget that shit. Wanted to bust you in the head with something, but I knew I'd better stay clear of you, cause if anything happened I was gonna ride the beef. What happened to you anyway Cain? You went to school and everything, I'd a been made if I were you, stead of being out here like I am now."

I was king. To whom all good things were to come. But here we are, together, reduced to the same thing. Me, whose expectations were great. Used to envy Lolly as a child, his freedom and adult manner, he was never a child. A ten-year-old who stayed out all night and didn't go to school when he didn't want to and drank wine. He grew up funny, always an old man, no different now than ten years ago, somehow skipping adolescence. On his own so early, he had no time for childish diversions or games. To support himself he gambled with the old men and preyed on women. Remember them talking about bad young Lolly in the barbershop when I was young. Fifteen years old in long shiny shoes with upturned toes, baggy silk pants, cashmere coats, and bald head, indistinguishable from the thirty- and forty-year-old men with whom he associated.

"Say, you know where we can get some girl, feel good, like partying. Got all this dope and money, gonna lay up for awhile."

"No."

"Let's get off again."

We cook up and hit again.

"Man, it feels good to have some money for a change. Don't have to get up in the morning sick and have to go out and hustle. Been so long, don't know how to act. But I been due, ain't had no breaks in a long time. What I'd really like to do is make one big sting. Say ten or twenty thousand. Could really take care of business. Wouldn't never be sick or have to hustle. Buy a piece of good stuff and put it on the street, some boss rags, a Cadillac, get a good woman, maybe open a little business. Yeah, I'd really take care of business. After I down these cameras should have some money. Bet nobody in my family, Mom, Pop, grandpeople ever had this much cash at one time in their lives. Yeah, tomorrow when I get straight, gonna buy some clothes, saw this leather down at Phil's for two bills, a suit, sharkskin or mohair, and I'm gonna sit up in the Gunsmoke and let everybody see me, buy everybody a drink, gonna be somebody for a little while. You be around tomorrow, down in the bar and watch. Dig Cain, wanna leave this trunk here a while till I find Sleepy. What's ever in it can wait. Be back tonight or tomorrow for it. Here's something for helping me."

He throws two bags of dope and a ten dollar bill at me and stumbles out. Sit on the bed fighting down an urge to run down the hall and mug him, take him off for everything he's got. He's so high he'd never know what happened. The unfairness of it all galls me. That he should have that money and no idea of what it can do for him, what he can do with it. He doesn't deserve it, so ignorant of the world and its pleasures, knowing no more than the street corner he was born on and will die on. Thinking the world begins and ends on 64th Street. Would never occur to him to walk across the street to Lincoln Center or to take a trip out of this place and leave it all behind, begin anew somewhere else. Clothes, Cadillacs, women, money and more money, another king for a day, he'll be greasy as ever next week, out there exactly as he began, with nothing. I forget him, pocket the money, shoot a bag and sit debating to open the trunk or not.

It's a good trunk, got to be something valuable inside. A treasure of some sort. Money, that's what it is, money. I know it, sure as anything, it's a trunk full of money. Look around for something hard to pry it open with, the silverware just bends. Tip down the hall and get the pipe. The thought of this money, can't keep my hands from shaking, so shoot my last bag for calm and strength. Using the pipe like a crowbar send the lock flying across the room and raise the lid.

I dig through the pile of books and struck by the sight of money, get vertigo and my knees buckle. Snatching a bill, hold it to the light, smell it, taste it, crumple some and put it in my pocket. It's real money, more than I can count or reason about. Like those figures in the paper of stock exchanges and millionaires' income. That's not the same money that you and I slave forty hours a week for and can buy so little with. It's not the same thing, but some other rate of exchange used by fictitious people out of fairy tales, but it couldn't be dollars. If it was, how could any one person have so much of it and so many so little? Taking more bills, I stick them in my pockets and run to the window to see if Lolly has gone. Watch him get into a cab on the avenue. Slam the trunk and throw it on my back and hit the streets.

WHERE CAN I TAKE IT? Not home, too many explanations. Nichole's house. Hail a taxi and head downtown.

Walking to the building think of what I'll say. Saw her the other day for the first time in four years when I took Sabu home.

Her nosy Italian neighbors crowd the stoops, grandmothers gossiping in Italian while their grandchildren run around screaming American curses. Used to hate them in their black clothes, Catholicism and death. Always hanging around like bad luck. They watch me suspiciously as I stand in the lobby searching the directory for her bell. Got to get off the streets this trunk is making me hot.

"Daddy George?"

Sabu smiles up at me and opening the door with a key on a string round her neck, she leads upstairs and runs inside the apartment.

"Mommy. Daddy George is here."

"George. George, how're you. Come on in. What's that you've got?"

"Hey baby how're you. Do me a favor? Let me leave this trunk here for a while. Got to see my P.O. in an hour. Talk to you when I get back."

"You can put it in the room."

I drag it into the room, snatch some money and push the trunk under the bed.

"I got some important things in there, papers and what not. Don't let Sabu get to it. Be back this evening."

"Let me give you this extra set of keys, may not be here when you get back."

She goes through a drawer and comes up with the keys, handing them to me with a look I know.

IV

RIDING THE SUBWAY to the bus depot, dreams fill my head, I am rich, and can do anything. At 42nd catch a bus for Newark. We pull in downtown Broad Street, place full of shoppers and workers going about their business. The TV and news reports must've been a dream, see no blood-splattered pavements, broken windows or angry mobs. But again there is the hate I felt when visiting my people. Not till I reach Springfield Avenue do I see the marks of rebellion. Blackened storefronts, glass and broken goods litter the streets. The air stinks burnt and damp from fire and water. I walk through, the whole avenue to myself. Where is everyone, have they packed them off to detention centers in the country? At high noon Springfield is a ghost town. Turning around, I head for the courthouse. It's early, and having an hour before my appointment, I sit up in the courtroom watching the proceedings.

The stage and setting are familiar, white-haired judge, dark wood paneled theater, ever-present flag and eagle, jurors, lawyers and D.A.'s. Begin sweating, my stink fills my nose and the courtroom.

"You George Cain have been found guilty of murder."

The prosecutor jumps up and screams, "Guilty," and points gleefully at me, my defense whispers the word in my ear—"Guilty." I hear but don't feel anything, am drained of everything, there is nothing they can do or take from me. The spectators and jury rise at a sign and chant in unison, "Guilty, guilty."

Tapping gavel brings order. Looking down, the judge says, "Have you anything to say before I pass sentence?"

Can see the place, its furnishings, light subdued coming from somewhere overhead, the smiling faces. Smiling at the knowledge of their righteousness, belief in this justice they administer. Faces eager, expectant, ears up like animals to hear my guilty words. They watch me, waiting for a sign, a gesture, a bursting hate-filled tirade, a begging remorseful cry, anything to justify them who sit in judgement. But there is nothing. Am sad, an infinite sorrow which silences. Nothing, except the all answering silence.

Run from the courtroom to a toilet, lock myself in. Vomiting and sick with need. Cook up shaking all the while. Hit and blackness.

A banging on the door wakes me and I snatch the dropper of coagulated blood from my arm. "Be out in a minute."

I clean the mess and stumble into the empty marble halls. Another near fatal O.D., but always I return from the dead to try again, my life is always on the line. Hesitate outside the office. My voice and eyes will betray me. Put on my shades, check for bloodstains and walk in. The receptionist takes my name.

"Mr. Romo will be out in a minute."

I'm trying to collect myself when he comes out.

"Hello George. How're you? Come on into the office."

I follow, stumbling to regain balance.

"Have a seat. Smoke? Well how's it going? Haven't been able to get in touch with you, you're never home. Guess your father told you I called. Nice man, your father. You're lucky, he's very concerned about your welfare. You're living at home? Your father couldn't tell me, understand he's only there on weekends. Very intelligent man.

"You know you're not to leave the state without first calling to get permission, even if it is just across the river. How long have you been on parole? You know the rules better than that. You were born there and all your friends are there? You can make new friends out here. That's what you need, your former associates are what got you in trouble in the past.

"You like sports. You know the YMCA downtown? I go two nights a week myself. You can always meet people there, they give dances and socials. You're not too old to make new friends and it'd be good for you, the exercise and everything. Build yourself up, look like you're losing weight since the last time I saw you. Try it? Good, good, know you'll enjoy it. Some nice people there, tell them I recommended you.

"So now what about your living at home? You don't want to? Why not? You're a man now. So what's that got to do with any- thing? You pay rent don't you? Just as if you were living some- where else. It helps them too, why shouldn't they get the money? That doesn't make sense, you're a man so you can't live at home. There isn't any friction between you and your family, is there? You knew one of the conditions of your release was that you would reside at home and you did agree to that. Can't possibly see what your being a man and living at home have got to do with one an- other. Sure I can see if you said a woman every now and then, I understand that and don't mind your staying out once in a while, we're all human."

The words are useless, he doesn't understand a thing I say. I understand him only because I have to to survive and every word from his mouth is a brick in the wall between us.

"Are you working? When do you plan to start? Really now, you've been back long enough to have gotten a job. You talk about being a man? Well act like one, a man must work. You think I or anybody else wants to work? Of course not, but we're men and we have duties and responsibilities."

I listen to this fool ranting about a job, what do I need with a job, got more money than he's ever seen and he talks about a job.

"Look, Mr. Romo. Why don't you can that shit, just let me fill out the forms each month and stop bothering me. My mother gets tired of you calling and I don't like the idea of you upsetting her with inquiries and threats of what you can do to me, she got enough troubles without that. I'm three times seven and don't need anybody telling me how to live this one, you ain't my father."

Hurt by my ingratitude, he continues, "Sorry you feel that way George. Had thought of us as friends and I'm only looking out for your benefit. You should see how some of the other officers work, they don't care what a man does, long as he sends in the forms and doesn't get arrested. But I care about you, I go out of my way to help. That's what I'm here for, to help you and anything less than that would not be doing my job. I know how you feel about your arrest and the law. But I had nothing to do with that, I don't make the laws and until they're changed there is nothing to be done. This riot should teach you something. I sympathize with your people but they must seek redress through the courts. Things will change. You're intelligent, you can see that George. And the same applies to you. You're high right now I bet."

"Yes I'm high."

"You know that's grounds enough for violation. How long you been doing it?"

"Since the day I got back. That was the first thing I did."

"Why do you do this to yourself? You want me to violate you? You want to go back to jail? Don't you George? It was easy there, three squares and a bed, somebody always telling you what to do, no responsibility? It's too tough out here for you. Some kind of man, can't cope with life. What's the problem George? Tell me and we can work it out."

"You whitey, you're my problem."

"That's not fair George. Be reasonable, you're intelligent, how can you say that, categorically saying all whites are bad. That's prejudice and that's wrong."

"It isn't prejudice, I didn't prejudge you people. I lived and watched you and I know what my problem is better than you." Hearing myself and the frustration of not being understood make me see how crazy this is.

"Well, looking through your record it doesn't seem as if whitey did you any harm. Scholarships to the best private schools and colleges in the country. Your family has a higher income than mine. On your first arrest you were given special consideration because of the testimony of a white clergyman. You had it better than most, white or black, so I don't see where you can talk about 'whitey.' What's ever been done to you that you didn't bring on yourself?"

"You know so much about how good whitey's been to me. Maybe you can tell me why. Why did he treat me so good, why did he tell me that I was different from the others, why did he fill me with all that shit of his, why?"

"I don't like that word whitey, wish you wouldn't use it. I respect you as an individual. Please show me the same courtesy. I don't know why they gave you so much or what they did to you, but why indict me for something in the past? This is today and I want to help you, let me."

"I told you what you could do. Leave me alone. Other officers only ask that you fill out the forms and stay out of trouble. I can do that if you leave me alone. Stop taking such an interest. I'm gonna do what I want to anyway. You know I'm no criminal, so what are you going to do, violate me, send me to the penitentiary? You're interested in my welfare, act like it."

"I agree, you're not a criminal and prison isn't the place for you, but what am I to do? You tell me. Let you go along doing what you're doing until you're dead of an overdose, then I share the blame, cause I knew and if I'd done my job could've prevented it. I got to sleep at night too and I've got a job to do."

"Who am I hurting? Ain't hit nobody over the head. This ain't nobody's business but mine."

"Well something's got to be done. You say you're not hooked. I'm going to make an appointment for you at Pines Hospital. They have facilities for detecting narcotics in the body. We've worked with them before and they're good people. I'll make the appointment for the end of the week. That will give you time to dry out. If you don't keep this appointment, I'll have no alternative but to think that you are hooked and no longer in control and shall have a warrant for your arrest taken out. I'm not fooling with you George. Now that that's over, why don't you stay and talk. Tell me what you think of this riot."

"Ask yourself."

I've hurt him, his fallen face shows it. Brush past his extended hand and out of the office. How do I feel about the riot, what kind of question. . . . Like asking a dead man is he dead. How are you supposed to feel?

RIDE BACK TO THE CITY wondering what possessed me. Made me carry on like crazy. Know he won't violate me. Chump really thinks he can help somebody, faggot ass M.F. needs to help himself. Why don't he leave me alone?

Prison. Its memory sobers. Got to be clean for that examination. Takes seventy-two hours to dry out. Got five days. Plenty of time. The money begins working its magic, throttling the monkey. It cures. Am secure, calm, no anxiety about the next moment—it shall pass without illness. Money insulates me from life. No longer must I throw bare soul against the machine. Money eases the pain and keeps me from the edge. Not since prison have I felt this free from need, from throwing that brick. Know now how artificial my desperation is. All my problems are created by the time and place I live in.

Take the bus downtown to Washington Square. Walking across the park see strange signs and omens. Young white beggars fill the streets, pawing and panhandling. Dirty and drugged. Everywhere gross acts and running obscenities. Bold, they exhibit their infirmities for sympathy and inspection, dead souls and lost minds. The cancer has found a fatter host, it began somewhere deep in my bowels and now consumes America. Tourists roam the place. Laughing and giving freely for what they think funny, not knowing it is their own death they're watching.

Coming onto Thompson Street, go into my bag. I swagger and sneer at them. Italian women dressed in dumpy black, hanging from the windows and stoops, cursing me in their foul tongue while counting beads and blessings.

Climb the stairs wondering why have I come back to this place, a woman I haven't seen in years and child I don't know. Make up my mind to leave, find a place somewhere. Got money. Fuck the parole, I'll take a trip, buy things, they'll never find me. Stand listening outside the door wondering what we'll say after all these years. The house is quiet. Her note on the table says to meet them at the playground. Think about leaving right now, but it's too late in the day. Check the trunk and the money and go down laughing at her.

"The playground," a reference to our common history, that

time to which she intends to tie us again, using the child as her agent. How can she know I hate her, hate that time and have returned only to see how far I've gone. She and that history are only a point of departure from where I can see my progress and evolution. Coming out the building bump into them and Nichole performs for the eager Italians watching and straining to hear while Sabu confused hides in herself.

"Hello George, how're you? Look who's here Bu. Your Daddy George has come to see you."

Bu smiles and takes my hand.

"See how she loves her father." Nichole talks loudly for the audience. The whisperers she calls them. All these years they've laughed knowing there wasn't a father around. They thought it fit punishment for one so shameless, living with black men. The Lord had punished her and to think this parable had been acted out before their eyes, not so it could be forgotten and its moral lost. Nay, a story they would elaborate and tell far and wide as evidence of God's will.

From dawn to dusk whispering about what goes on, while their rude brats run around cursing and howling. The men, fathers and husbands to these people, lusting fools with drunken eyes, are no better. Coarse and brutish, all-American, wishing us dead, especially the child. She's testimony to what I've done. Egged on by grog, friends and family, how often have they baited me and come so near dying? Put my hands on Nichole and fondle her. She smiles. Her stupidity irks me and I slap her. The sound raises the men. They move as if to do something. Dare them with my eyes and they turn away. I'm gratified by the intense hatred this generates around us. It's a contest between me and them and I always win.

Have only to touch Nichole and she thinks I want her, unchanged since I saw her last. It's as if I'd never gone. There is nothing to say, she will not believe and doesn't want to hear what she already knows. I left because I hated her.

"I'm sorry baby."

Kiss her on the forehead and squeeze her for them, she smiles and all is well.

"Don't you love your father?" Nichole repeats to make sure they've heard her.

"Let's go to the store, ain't nothing upstairs to eat."

"You got money George?"

"All you want."

"Daddy George got money? Buy me a toy?"

Throw Bu on my shoulder and Nichole takes my waist to spite the world. Once off Thompson, feel the tension leave as I slide back into anonymity. My color, beard, white woman and half-breed child attract little attention. Even the police on every corner ignore us, we're a common sight in the Village proper.

We meet friends of Nichole's in the market and she introduces me as Sabu's father. They act as if I were a dirty word. Wonder what she's told them. Buy Bu a doll to quiet her and she goes outside to play.

Five minutes later she asks me to come out with her. Leading me by the hand, takes me outside to meet a pack of half-breed children like herself. "This is my father. He brought me this doll."

They look at me strangely, trying to cipher the cryptic statement. "You really her father?" one boy asks. There's something wrong with these kids, can see it in their eyes, they lack innocence and I feel uncomfortable. Nichole calls me to come help her and rescues me from their gaze. Walking away hear them talking.

"That's not her father."

"Yeah, he's just another man."

Turn around to glimpse them again. One kid makes an obscene

gesture and goes tearing down the street. Pay for the groceries and head back to the pad.

"Who're those kids?"

"The children from the playground, friends of Bu's. You met most of their mothers in the store."

Begin to understand. Those kids, products of the integration time, trapped by black awareness. It took their mothers' lovers, their fathers, leaving bitterness. Remember the chicks she introduced me to, they were all white, American and for some reason Jewish. Wonder if Nichole has switched allegiance after being burned by so many blacks. When I had her, she was nigger struck and couldn't stand her people.

By the time we get back it's dark and the audience has departed to eat. Spot one or two spying from blacked out windows. For them Nichole has an obscene gesture. We laugh going up the stairs. She must think it's like old times, we versus the world.

Once we thought we were different, not black or white, something unique, special. Why couldn't everyone be like us? There'd be no race or any other problems. Arrogance and blind stupidity. We were two racists living together, knowing only the myth of each other, speaking a language of homonyms. From such different places with different ways, we offended and didn't know we did and by the time it was over, the myth had become reality.

ROGER, A PREVIOUS WHITE LOVER OF NICHOLE'S, made it all so clear. He came by the pad often. Ingratiating himself and maintaining contact with her for the time I'd leave and he could return. I tolerated him for his lavish gifts and attention. He'd been bugging me to get him some smoke from uptown and desperate for money I agreed. Knowing enough of the game he insisted that he accompany me. Explained why he couldn't, a white in Harlem is a tip. Police know what he's up there for, pussy or dope and all they got to do is lay. It didn't matter, was going to beat him anyway. He stood on the corner, I took the bread, turned the corner and kept on going. Partied the money and returned a week later, broke. Roger had already seen her and told what had happened.

Shouldn'tve been no big thing, had been stealing and taking from her regular, though she said nothing and pretended it didn't happen. Rather than force a confrontation, she'd leave more money for me to take. So guilty, she indulged and tried to understand my every weakness, making me weaker and more dependent. Hated her understanding and insistence on thinking she understood. That all we had to do was talk about it, communicate and somehow it'd all work out. She couldn't understand how things and incidents unrelated to us in any way should have such profound effects on our relationship. She loved me and my attitude changed with the fortunes of my people in the pages of the *Times*.

"Why can't we go somewhere?"

Couldn't even then be seen with her outside the Vil.

"Why don't you bring your friends by? This is your home too."

It was her home. I only slept there because I had no place to go.

"What's wrong, tell me baby? Talk to me."

We were wrong. She knew but wouldn't let go, trying to suck me of all strength. So weak and near drowned, hooked and in need of money, I couldn't leave. Complying with my degradation I stayed and sunk deeper.

"George why'd you do it? Why'd you steal that money from Roger? If you want money, you know all you have to do is ask. Why'd you steal?"

"Steal what? Didn't steal anything. What you talking about?"

"You know what I'm talking about. That money you got from Roger for the smoke."

"Didn't steal it, I beat him. He gave it to me."

"You stole it, you admit stealing it."

"Didn't steal anything, I beat that fool, can't you understand that?"

"All I know is you took that money. You stole, stole, stole!"

Tried to explain, but there was no understanding in her eyes and I saw the futility, she could never understand.

"Roger called and told me what happened, said to tell you if you didn't give back the money he was calling the police and telling them you stole something from his house. Told him I'd take care of it soon as I saw you."

Hearing this, rage took me and I screamed, "He said he'd do what? Call that punk, what's his number. I'll kill him. You give him a penny and I'll break your hands.

"Hello Roger? This is George."

"Nichole tell you what I said? You got my money?"

"She told me what you said. Now listen to what I say. You punk motherfucker, you call the police, cause you gonna need one. I'll kill you! You hear me faggot! I'll kill you, bust a cap in your ass!"

Was screaming, heard him swallow and try to find his tongue.

"You, you . . . You're just like the rest of them. Thought you . . ."

Couldn't believe it, didn't want to, not what he was saying. Thought I was like him. Why? Cause I went to school and M.F. wasn't every other word. Forgot the nigger was just beneath the veneer of civilization.

"That's right, I'm just like them. What the fuck did you think I was? Like you faggot? And I carry a knife in my pocket just like all of them and I'm gonna take your head. You gonna call the police on somebody. Where do you think you're at? Just what the fuck you call yourself doing?"

"I'm sorry man, ain't calling the police, just trying to scare you into giving my money back."

Fear in his voice, heard the bitch coming out of him cross the wire, "Really man, I'm not calling the police."

"You better not. And don't be bothering her trying to get any money, she didn't take it. I took it. I took it, you dig that. And if you want it, you got to see me."

"I'm sorry man."

The bitch in him disgusted me and I slammed the phone down surprised at how easy it was. All he'd done was whimper, no challenge, nothing. Still couldn't believe he intended to call the police. Did he think they could protect him in my world? When he put that money in my hand, he willingly crossed over and became subject to the laws of another place. If he got a gun or knife and came to get his scratch I'd a upped it, but to call the police.... His arrogance in thinking he could remove an act from the context in which it occurred and put it in his world. Typical of those people. Was glad I'd beat him, he deserved it. He made himself a victim. Not everybody is, only those who let themselves be. Every mark gives himself away. Thugs lay hours in shadows till a victim makes himself available. They let others obviously more prosperous pass till that right one comes along. What gives him away? He knows in advance that it is to be him. His eyes show fear and fear betrays him. Roger knew he was going to be a victim in advance, whoever he dealt with would have known and done him the same.

"Why did you steal George?"

Knowing she was bothering me she persisted and more clearly I began to see how distant and incompatible we were.

"Look, I told you I didn't steal anything, but you don't believe me or understand so why don't we drop it?"

"But I want to. Just explain to me."

"Look baby, if I got to explain it to you, you can't understand it."

"But you took his money and you didn't give him anything. You just took his money. What if he'd called the police. They'd have taken you to jail."

"What do they know about anything I do or why. You're supposed to be my woman and you can't understand a thing."

"Don't say that George. I do, you know I try to but it's hard sometimes."

From that moment I began to consolidate my dissipated strength to break away. My hate and loathing had finally overcome my need. Would simply leave one morning and never come back, no fanfare. Would not have to kill her, as I had thought, to escape from the devil, would just cut out.

IT'S LATE AND BU FALLS ASLEEP over her plate. While Nichole readies her for bed, I get off again. Sit nodding on the toilet remembering how we met. Met her at a civil rights fundraising party that turned into a drunken revel. She was like me, alone. Supposed to meet a friend, but the friend hadn't come so we sat drinking and staring vacantly. She was tired, having spent the day ringing doorbells and handing out flyers for the organization. Would I take her home? In the street I hailed a cab.

"It's too far and much quicker by subway."

At first balked at the idea, not wanting to be seen with a white woman and prey to rude eyes. Waiting on the platform, she took my hand. I wanted to pull away and leave, but instead returned the pressure and enjoyed offending the onlookers. Leaving the subway began to dread the moment. Didn't know how to be with her. Wanted to get away, was sick and needed a fix. We kissed quickly at her door and I ran fast as I could to shoot it away with stuff.

Was prowling the streets and bumping through crowds, annoyed cause I hadn't found something to steal. Had been days since I'd spoken a word. Wanted to talk, to anyone. A week had passed since we'd met and pushed each other from mind. Fumbling through my pockets for something, came across her number on a matchbook and called her.

"Who's this?"

"Cain, George Cain. Met you at the party last week."

Silence as she tried to recall me. Then she began speaking as if we were intimates, telling me every detail of her miserable life. Was wary of this confidence, but soon enjoying it. We talked until the operator interrupted, promising to meet later that evening.

I prepared myself for the encounter by stopping at Sun's for a fix and arrived late. Spotted her on 14th Street and Seventh Avenue. The severe cut of clothes and butch haircut gave her an air of ice-cold efficiency. She couldn't love anything or anybody. Strangers, we greeted each other awkwardly and took a cab uptown. Feeling loose from dope, I told her about the streets and things I thought she understood. But to her it was all a surreal nightmare.

The restaurant was in the Seventies. Took her there knowing we wouldn't be bothered or see anyone I knew. She told me about herself, the protest movements she was involved in, civil rights, ban the bomb, abortion reform, and numerous magazines and articles she read. All of her time and energy was devoted to the gathering of information. During the day she was a writer for one of the press services. She lived in the dead yesterday of news reports or the tomorrow of reform. The pressing moment never intruded till I came and drove her into life.

We finished dinner and walked by the river, my river. I led her through the park to its edge, remembered swimming in it.

"Why so quiet?"

"I use to swim here."

"It's dirty isn't it?"

"I suppose so."

She looked out over the water. I kissed her. The mouth was dead.

"What's the matter?"

"Nothing."

"Something must be, you acting so funny. You don't dig niggers or something?"

She grabbed my hand pushed it under her skirt and pressed it between her thighs. Sucked tongue in her mouth and squeezed. Felt myself grow big and bust.

We rode the train in silence. It would happen that night, would finally get over. Unlike the first time, I'd prepped myself. Leaving the subway, she handed me the keys to her place.

"GEORGE. You okay in there?"

"Yeah baby, be out in a minute." Clean up and stash the guns.

"Your daughter wants you to kiss her good night."

Ending her prayers, Sabu jumps up and kisses me. "Night Daddy George. You'll be here when I wake Daddy? You won't go away?"

"I'll be here baby."

"See how she misses you? You should stay in touch George. She's like that all the time. Asking about you, how come you don't come see her."

In the dark I fumble with her clothes. She undresses us and the naked flesh releases torrents. Everything in me, all the poison, bursts in her. A quick hurtling down. What more could there be? It is drained of all pleasure by the countless times of dream and thought in prison. She snuggles to me like an animal content and grateful that I've scratched its belly and given it pleasure.

"Oh baby I missed you. Missed you so bad. I love you, don't leave me alone like that. I need you."

Cannot believe my ears, she acts like I've been gone a day, not four years and everything is the same. Sitting on the side of the bed, know I hate this woman. Loathe her, her whiteness, her love. Whenever I touched her, would wash and walk for hours in the air and still her scent clung. Her love is like that, a tenacious clinging thing, choking me to death. Could've killed her easily, with pleasure.

Looking at the dumb face, see how it has changed. Before me, she had no life, that is why she's grateful. She got no mail cept statements from the bank and magazines. Her phone was dusty and rang only wrong numbers. She had no friends and never went out. To work and home to the papers, books and magazines. Her involvement in groups was as an anonymous member. She was dead and I resurrected her, at great cost, and that is why I never felt guilty about nothing cause it was my due. Twenty-eight years and she'd not loved, crying and shamed at herself and pleasure the first time, thinking she was a nympho. Had no inkling what love was about. I was amazed that she could have opinions and attitudes about everything and still hadn't fulfilled her primary function. I made her into a woman to meet my needs.

Now there's neither love nor hate. The whiteness no longer excites me, it's nothing and she's nothing. As whenever I make a great discovery, or change because I find some new truth about life, feel something heavy that constricted my mind leave and know I'm closer to freedom. Understanding of self and proper awareness and action in life is freedom for me. The Man can't free me. I must free myself.

Touch her and feel nothing, no revulsion. Wonder if I could ever love her or any of them and know I couldn't. Not because of their whiteness, but because of what being white makes you. Lay back down and sleep.

A RACKET IN THE KITCHEN wakes me. Hear Sabu, Nichole and another voice. My stirring around attracts their attention.

"What do you want for breakfast?"

"Eggs and cereal."

It is 10:00, too late to look for a pad, another day shot. In the bathroom take my wake up and wash, wondering who's in the kitchen. A young blond thing greets me.

"Hi Cain, remember me? Chris?"

I rummage in memory. Chris the kid next door. Years ago.

"Remember her George? She was just a baby last time you saw her."

"Yeah I remember. How you been? Look at you now, something else."

Smiles and blushes. "Didn't think you'd remember. Glad you're back. Everybody missed you."

While eating, Nichole bothers me with attention. So insecure, every female is a threat and Chris, sixteen years old, is no exception. Finish, get ready to leave. Hear Chris in the kitchen.

"I told him if he couldn't wait, screw off and get someone else. After that I went with Ray, he thought he was slick and went out with Grace on the sly. I don't have to tell you why, you can imagine. She had his kid and they got married. Two months later he calls me and says, 'Look Chris, I love you and I want to divorce

Grace.' Told him he was crazy and hung up. Barry, my new boy-
friend, got married when he was young. They're separated now.
His wife's a bitch, only lets him see the baby for a few hours on
weekends."

Picture Nichole moving around the kitchen amused at this
young girl's problems that were never her own. Chris's love life,
free, careless, adolescent. Tales of fantasy touching nothing that
I'm familiar with.

"I'm going out for a while, be back tonight."

"Okay baby. Be careful."

"You going by subway?" Chris asks. "I'm going that way."

Nichole gives her a woman's look and we leave. Watch Chris
play woman with me and other males. Playing, not prepared to be
one. Can't imagine those cats she fucks over, how can they stand
for something like that, serves them right if they go for it.

"What you been doing with yourself Chris? Sure looking
good."

"Nothing much, parties and things."

"Still take care of Bu for Nichole?"

"Yeah, I dig her. She's like my sister, spend so much time with
her. Nichole's always out somewhere."

Walk the rest in silence.

"See you tomorrow George?"

"Later baby." Can smell virgins, they're unnatural creatures.
Suddenly I remember, this is the last day I can get off, got to
be clean for that exam Friday. Take the train to 125th. Wander
in and out of clothing stores trying on everything and buying
nothing.

Am habit bound, been so long since I spent money on things,
am unable to part with it except for dope. Buy some socks and
underclothes and ride downtown feeling like a native who's just
spent his first money. Cannot believe I got something in return

for it. Something real, that will not vanish like a feeling. I can look at it a week from now and say so much money went there and have something to show for it.

AT 59TH STREET get off and go around the way. Going to sit up in the bar, high side, buy a few drinks, be somebody for a while. Hit the projects from the downtown side where all the spics be. Know them all, grew up with em, went to the same schools, did the same things. Stand rapping with Lopez a while and this chick pushing a baby gives me a look. Catch her halfway down the block all set to say something slick and she turns to me.

"Don't remember me, do you, Georgie Cain?"

Look closely, take age from around the face, a little flesh from the body, put woman's knowledge out of her eyes and pain from her smile.

"Nandy, Nandy. Baby how're you?" We dance joyously in the street, no longer strangers, sweet memories springing immediately in my head.

"How've you been? Oh you look so good, let me hug you again."

"Girl, who made you so fine!"

"Go on, you know you can't run no games on me. Remember? This is little sister."

"I told you then I was going to wait for you. This you?" I pick the child up. Can tell by her tone, proud and defiant that she has no husband.

"This my heart here. Tchaka."

"How old is he?"

"Four months."

"Four months? Big, another warrior. Go head sister. I know he's gonna be ready and know who he is."

"You know that."

"Which way you going? Home? Still there? I'll walk you."

Walking through the project pass acquiantances from the underground. Recognizing she is not one of us, they either salute me with unusual courtesy or privately not wanting to pull me down through association with them. For many of them, unknowing they're victims, believe the myth that they're the lowest of low, and give it reality. That mad need to punish and destroy ourselves is past, our minds and bodies are needed. We are free if we want to be.

"What you doing tonight? Feel like going out?"

"Going where? Ain't been out in so long."

"A flick, dancing, a club, anything."

"I got to work in the morning."

"We won't be out late. Come on. I haven't seen you all this time."

"Okay. What time?"

"How long will it take you? I'm going like this."

"Well I've got to feed Tchaka and eat."

"No, we'll eat out."

"Let me see if I can get my sister to keep him. Be ready in an hour."

"Pick you up in an hour then." Help her in with the carriage and Mrs. Wood greets me with a kiss.

"How've you been boy? How's the family? Your mother? Haven't seen her in ages. And the boys. How they doing? Staying out of trouble? Good, good, everybody's fine. Lord bless em. You got to excuse the house, but it's so crowded here with all the kids running round."

There's tension between these women. Want to leave. Nandy understands and hurries me out.

"I'll see you in an hour." She brushes my lips closing the door.

Walk into the air, my insides screaming to be near her. Am so free near that young girl, clean, that's how I felt. Clean. From filth and decay, all the abstractions and bullshit. She's real.

Race through the projects to Fat Man's house. Need a fix.

IN THE ELEVATOR, the hall, on the stairs, see the litter of junkies coming and going, burnt glassine sacks curled like black caterpillars, burnt matches and bloodstains. Knock and hear the children scurrying about to push a chair to the peephole.

"It's Mr. George."

"Let him in girl."

Rose, nine years, the oldest, lets me in and the others come running up. Calling Mr. George, eyes bright, expectant, knowing I never come without something for them. They line up by age, each giving his name as I put a coin in his hand. Can never remember them all. Sister's in the kitchen tending pots, looking more tired than I've ever seen her.

"How're you Sister? Everything okay? Don't look well."

"Tired, tired, that's all. Just stay tired, can't do nothing. Maybe I start taking some of that dope ya'll use to give me some energy." She smiles and I wonder how. The pain.

"Rosie come here. Okay Sister, how's my girl been?"

"Rosie's always good. She don't give me no trouble. Looks after the house, take care of the kids, helps cook dinner. She's good, except she don't like to go to school sometimes when I don't feel too good or Howard's real sick."

Rosie smiles and I see my helplessness in outraged clarity, no matter what I give or do her, it's wasted. She will not survive. The unfairness of it is crazy, condemned to death before she was born. How could they bring her into life without hope or chance? Generous and frustrated give Sister twenty and stick five in Rosie's hand.

"Do something for yourself Rosie, this is yours, all yours. You hear?" To have a chance, she must be selfish.

"All this George?"

"Don't kick it around Sis, but I finally made that big sting."

"Thanks George. Thanks."

"Where's Fat?"

"Howard's in the room, want me to call him?"

"No, I'll go on back."

Walk into a carcass-strewn cave where the hunted huddle around a TV watching cartoons. A glow shows the half-nude children, retarded and otherwise, playing over the bodies, junkies nodding, stinking, burning, high. How do they stand themselves? Immune to their ever-present foulness. Call Fat. His head comes out the dark, skin strapped tight around the skull, eyes running, gaunt and hollow, body a black thread. Sweat pours off him and he shakes with need, begging and whining like he's going to die.

"Say man, do something for me, I'm sick Cain, look at me, help me. Do something for me. Can't stand it."

He is always sick, there's not enough stuff in the world to quash his need.

"Who's got it?"

"Curtiss in there on the floor got something nice. What you want?"

"Get me a half."

His eyes light with anticipation almost human. "I'll cop for you, wait here."

Give him the scratch. Hear Curtiss mumble as Fat begs him for an extra bag. Lock ourselves in the bathroom, fix and sit nodding till one of the kids has to use the toilet. Straighten up and go into the kitchen with Sister while Fat cleans up. Sitting in a broken chair, I tell her news of the outside world. Except for the

TV and the Jehovah's Witnesses, I'm her only link with it and her interest welcomes conversation.

"Have you been to Lincoln Center?"

Tell her about the place, marble bathroom, carpeted halls, chandeliers and works of art. Clinging to every word, she transports herself and closing her eyes moves in the elegant surroundings. Rosie and the other girls have taken seats and listen enthralled, never having penetrated the marble tomb across the street.

"We have tickets to go next week, they gave them out in school." Then disappointed, "But we can't go."

Sister cuts Rosie with a look. The session is over and the children go back to their corners.

"How come you're not going Sis?"

"I ain't never been anywhere like that, wouldn't know how to act, got nobody to go with."

"When is it?"

"Saturday afternoon."

"How many tickets you got?"

"It's free, but Howard won't go."

"How about if I went with you?"

"Have to ask Howard."

Fat comes lurching into the room all high and attentive. "Have to ask me what?"

"If I can take them to Lincoln Center Saturday."

"Sure, yeah, didn't know you went for that stuff. But you always was a funny nigger."

"Just thought be nice to go inside, see what it's like. Ain't you curious?"

"I been in there stealing and whatnot, but never to see no show. Couldn't sit still for no shit like that."

The children have come from their corners to beg him. "Can we go Daddy?"

"You promise to behave and don't be no trouble."

They applaud and scatter not giving him a chance to change his mind. Sis smiles grateful and Fat pleased with himself goes on back to the room.

"What time's the show?"

"Two-thirty."

"I'll be by at one then, give everybody plenty of time to get ready."

"Have to get my dress together, Rosie's, Denise, shine the boys' shoes." Sis goes on dreaming, escaping the dreary moment, lost in the details of preparation and anticipation and am grateful at having given her a moment's respite. Looking around I note the sticks of furniture, nothing in the house is worth a two dollar bag. Fat done sold everything of value to feed the monkey. Remembering this is the last day I can get off, give him five bags, holding a couple in case.

"Okay everybody, got to go."

Riding downstairs smelling the diapers and stink clinging to me, am filled with warmth at the little happiness I've given. Remember Fat and Sister when they first came here from Mississippi. Had never seen anything like them. Fresh, vital and alive, but the city quickly took its toll, reducing them to their present state.

Transplanted sharecroppers living in an elevator building. There's no difference from here to there, hell is all the same.

NANDY IS WAITING on the stoop when I arrive. Seeing her the fog clears from my head and I'm madly in love.

Hail a cab and head downtown gripping her hand like a schoolboy. Not until we get out do I realize we're in the Vil. Be funny if we ran into Nichole. We eat at T.P.'s, laughing over drinks and the past. Cannot ignore the sense of freedom and cleanliness she gives me. Want to be good to her. Make her happy.

"You got an old man baby?"

"What you mean?"

"You know what I mean, some cat you dig, takes you out."

"Got a couple of em right now, but nothing serious."

Cannot hide my elation and she laughs. Laughter so pure and feminine. Everything about her is discovery. We go across the street and take the elevator downstairs to the jazz cellar. It's between sets and loud in conversation. Sit up in the gallery by the bandstand waiting for the group. Joint crowded with Ivy League whiteys and interracial couples. Rarely drink, grog don't agree with stomach or head, but after the third rum am feeling gay and the band comes on. It's a hard driving group and we can't be still for patting our feet. Intermission lights come on and I feel the eyes on her. Am drunk but able to decipher the lust in their look. She's the only sister in the place and all woman. She feels their eyes and scalds them with a hateful look.

"Niggers ain't shit."

"Say what?"

"Niggers ain't shit. Look at them with those devils, swear they into something. Can't see how ugly they are. Excuse me Georgie. I'm sorry but I can't help myself, makes me so mad to see one of us with them. It's nauseating and you can't tell them nothing. So smug, think they're together cause they got a white woman, a pig. A sister wouldn't put up with their shit. Half of em rejects from their own kind and a nigger runs behind them like a goddamn fool. Treat em better than he treat his own. Just makes me so mad. Be right back, going to the ladies' room."

Watch her go, turning heads. She's a queen, a sure enough queen, everybody in the place reacts to her. Her scorn is obvious and the niggers turn guiltily away to their white liberal lady friends commenting on the beautiful black woman that just went by. The men look and lust at her terrible blackness. They will not, cannot love her. Can't love what they've been taught to hate all their lives, nigger lips, red like fire in a black night, liquid brown eyes and nappy hair. She is beauty and acknowledged.

Looking about am struck by the ugliness of all the whites, suddenly, as if I had new eyes, had been blind all my life and now a miraculous restoration of sight. In an instant their hair, color, straight noses and grim lips always thought desirable are ugly. I see them for the first time like they really are. Free from the brainwash. How could my senses betray me like that? Or is it my mind that has betrayed my senses? Know I'm drunk and try to blink up on sobriety, but nothing will change my sight. Once again I feel some dark heavy weight lifting from my soul. Jump up and rush to the toilet to splash water in my face. Drying off I see him in the mirror watching me.

"Is she yours?"

"Is who mine?"

"That girl. Is she yours? How much do you want?"

Cannot believe my ears and think my senses have truly turned on me. Crazy things run in my brain, eyes bulge, mouth working and no sound coming out. See a stranger in the mirror.

Impatient he licks his lips and pulls his wallet out. "Come on, how much? I know she's a fine piece. I'll pay whatever you want, fifty, a hundred."

A pulse pounds hard and loud in my brain and ears, stomach muscles contract and tighten, taste the dope backing up in my throat before it spews out. Vomit on him. All in his face half-digested food and liquor, reeking and reeling he slips in it, eyes rolling wildly in his head. Laugh dangerously as I step over him wiping my mouth. When I get back she grips my arm and I share her contempt. The beautiful face set in an angry mask, challenging any bold enough to meet her eyes.

"Let's get out of here."

Crowd into the elevator full of whites, pressing and touching me all over. Breathing and filling the little space to suffocation. Hold my breath to prevent poisoning and pray for the stop. After an eternity, rush out gasping for air.

"Hate them, ooooh hate them I tell you, can't stand them people! See how those bitches looked at you? Do it all the time, got no pride, shame, nothing, animals and ugly as sin. Think they can get any black man, all they got to do is show their ass. What make it so bad, it's halfway true. Niggers just so weak, break a leg getting next to one of them tramps. Niggers just ain't no good, no way.

"Sorry baby, just sometimes I get so upset. You don't understand. I act stupid, but—you're from the city. Remember I'm from down South, lived most of my life down there and I know these people, know what they're like, what they've done to me and my people. Real things, not newspaper and TV. You're one of those artificial niggers. You had to learn to hate, what have they ever done to you? Nothing. You hate because of what you read, hear, you feel what you think you're supposed to feel. CBS, NBC programmed you to hate. My hate is a deep thing, part of me. It's there. I read the newspapers every day to see how many God has killed. It's hard for me to realize they're not going to hurt me. Come from a segregated place. When I came North and saw all this fuss about black, buy black, wanting black schools, black neighborhoods, I couldn't believe it. I'd gone to black schools most of my life, all the teachers, kids, principals were black. You did all your shopping in the district and we all lived together. I never saw blue eyes except in a magazine till I came here.

"When I first met you, thought you were the most stuck-up,

"Get yourself together nigger."

Set to thinking, this ain't Mississippi, it's New York. How can I beat the case? What can happen? Run around the kitchen looking for the liquor. Take a shot then empty the bottle. Throw five bags in the cooker and don't feel anything. Fuck it, they don't have a case, I'll just deny it, her word against mine, there were no witnesses, Bu don't know what happened. I'll go down on the stoop with her and wait for them. Another thought replaces that. Flee. Straight away and fast.

"Run nigger, run." Scramble around getting my money and run down into the streets. A police car speeds up sirens going and I duck into the hall knowing it's for me. Stand there heart beating like a drum and Bu's screams echoing in my ears. A cab lets Nichole out and I rush past her surprised face and jump in.

"Harlem, uptown anywhere!"

COMING DOWN AND OUT of stuff walk down Seventh looking to cop and run into J.B. He walks me to the snake pit. Pass Broadway, he smiles and nods as if nothing ever happened and comes over to us. Leery, I move the safety off the gun in my pocket.

"You hear Sun's out?"

"No. What happened?"

"They didn't find anything on him. Flower had it so they cut him loose. He's looking for you to help bail her out."

"Where's he at? Still downtown?"

"Her bail's one hundred cash, under alias Willa Mae Jones."

J.B. and I head back to the hotel.

"J.B., tell you Broadway tried to take us off the other day?"

"Say wha?"

"Yeah, him, Boy and Sugar. Niggers weren't playing either, ran me damn near downtown."

"Lolly was looking for you. Say you beat him for a sting he made."

"Yeah, he left a trunk down at the pad."

"What was in it?"

"Money."

"Man why don't you stop it?" he said in disbelief.

Get off and tell him what happened, Chris, the parole. Have to tell someone.

"Wow. You done really tore your ass, but ain't nothing going to happen. Broad probably won't say nothing and you can tell the P.O. something."

He's probably right. Push it from mind and stop worrying about it.

"Say Cain, I tell you your man C.J. died?"

"No. You jiving, not C.J. Just saw him couple days ago."

"Yeah, dead of an overdose. Found him on the roof in the projects."

Don't believe it. Just saw him alive. C.J. is dead. All my friends are dead or dying. The sacrificed generation, dropping like flies. The mortality rate is unbelievable, we're beating our fathers to the grave. None die of age, infirmity or make twenty-five. I'm one of the few survivors, alive at least. How can I believe I'll die tomorrow, when I'm young and alive now? C.J. was my best friend.

"Wonder if my mother knows, he was like a brother when we were kids. Always at each other's house. C.J. dead! What can we do J.B., they're killing all of us. We've got to stop it, warn the others."

"I know man. What's to do? You know it all Cain but it don't stop you. How you gonna stop it? You can't. You been around the way, all the kids are using stuff, young girls even, got it so there's one in every household using stuff. It's part of the Man's scheme, a way to keep a large part of the people helpless, an excuse for jailing and abusing them. Keep them so occupied they have no time to think and become a threat. It's the perfect weapon and they're not going to get rid of it."

Thinking of Sun and thousands of others, see the never ending spiral of addiction stretching years before me. Trapped in a prison of my own making which I walk around and carry wherever I go. More secure than bars and gun towers cause there's nothing outside. They don't need walls in Siberia, they're surrounded by untrackable expanses and freezing cold. Step off into it at your own risk.

Nandy. . . . Have got to talk, see her, she's the only way out. For her, I'll find a way out of this thing. Break the cycle.

It's always like this immediately after a fix and high. It's the last, always the last. Till I feel the hot cold flashes and pain in my back. I'm always full of sincerity and good intentions, but I never kick for good. Am comfortable with my illness, it's a part of me like another sense.

"Got to call Nandy. I'm gonna stop, J.B. Square business, I'm going to. Can't stand it anymore. I'm tired, so tired. Can't stand it, can't go on anymore."

"You got to show me. How many time you done kicked already, eight, nine, ten?"

"Got to call Nandy, let's go."

"Catch you later Cain."

He's cynical, cannot see the urgency or desperation. Want Nandy with me. Can't wait to get sick and feel the pain of recovery. Walk into the hotel and rent a room for the week and call her from the lobby.

"Nandy? Cain. Listen baby I need you. Now, right now. Something important's come up. In front of the Theresa."

While I wait, take a walk around, am going to kick. This time, no coming back and I want to see the place a last time this way. Know the world will turn when I'm through with this. Will see with different eyes. Just as before I used drugs I saw another way. There were morals, ethics, principles. Things I believed were right or wrong and after junk these things were no longer. But not only my mind, my senses became addled. Saw, heard, touched and behaved differently, was different. Looking up, see my feet have brought me to the snake pit, they knew no other direction. All around the business of the street goes on and I savor the camaraderie of the community of rejection a last time, then head back to the hotel. Am tired, so tired of the hassle, not the junk itself. If there were some way to continue without always suffering, I would. There's no pleasure, only pain. In the beginning at least I got high, but continued use brings only diminishing return. Use more and get less till the time when no amount will get you high or restore normalcy. You feel the rush and warmth for only a second, then begins the swift fall down, sick or always verging on illness, prey to police and your own kind. Everything's risky, a gamble. You take a chance stealing, then sell it for a fraction, get uptown and have to hunt down the bag. Even then you're not done, cause it might be a beat. Coming and going prey for everything and everybody, and the shit ain't nothing no way.

Spot Nandy a block away pacing in front of the hotel. Call to her and we hurry to each other. Seeing her fills me with resolution and strength.

"Oh baby worried to death about you. Got here quick as I could, you sounded so upset. What's wrong?"

"Let's go upstairs."

I fall on the bed and she sits beside me. "Last night I asked you to be my woman. Want to take care of you and Tchaka. I need you, but I can't do this without first telling you about me. Like I told you last night I've been in prison the last few years. I'm a junky baby. This is what I was sent away for. I'm on parole now and hooked again, the Man's talking about sending me back. Me

George Cain, I'm a dope fiend, you understand? A low-lifed M.F. Don't think I'm any different or better than the others. Just because I'm not dirty or greasy, cause I been that way. You know Fat Man, Lolly, Duke?"

She turns up her nose at the mention of these people, for they're the bottom of the world in her eyes.

"Well I'm just like them. One of them. I've stolen, lied, cheated, do anything for a fix just like them and until you showed didn't want to do it any other way. Had no reason to change. I want you Nandy, but I'm no good this way. Got to stop. Can't go to the hospital or one of those programs. Have got to do it myself and I can't do it without you. Need you with me for three days, need you every minute, can't be out of sight for any time cause I'm not strong enough without you. With you I can do anything and I'm asking you to save my life, our life together, cause there can't be anything for us if I'm this way. Nandy I'm asking for help, just stay with me till this is over."

Just like that, no questions, nothing. Already can feel her strength flow in me, preparing me for the ordeal ahead.

"What are you going to do about your job, Tchaka? I've got enough money to support us till I'm strong enough to take care of business."

"Got some time coming. I'll call in sick and my mother'll take care the baby. Don't worry about it. We'll have enough to do taking care of you. Better tell me what to expect."

"Had a fix this afternoon, won't be getting sick until morning. I'll vomit, sweat a lot, cry, nothing really way out."

"What do I do?"

"Just be here, that's all you can do, just be here and I'll do it. Eat yet? Might as well enjoy this little time we've left, let's eat out and go somewhere. Come on smile baby, this is a happy time, our life is just beginning."

We come out into a hot Harlem afternoon crowded with folk. A speaker holds forth on the corner making a plea for help for the victims of the Newark rebellion. Standing there holding Nandy's hand and watching the audience, mostly nodding junkies urging him on, feel a distance between me and them already. That bond which joined us is broken and I see them as they really are, no longer the chosen driven to destruction by their awareness and frustration, but only lost victims, too weak to fight. Walk downtown and I pull into '17th Street.

"Want to show you the place I was born in." The same people sit on the stoop and the same stickball game is in the middle of the street. The street so crowded with people and noise. I see it now, it's dirty, garbage, rats, roaches. All the romance is gone, don't want to live and die this way. Want more, better, a shot at life.

"I was born in that building twenty-three years ago."

"How do they live that way George? It's ugly, depressing. It's bad at home, down South, but it's different from this, better some way."

Walk up and down streets getting my last look at the place, and wherever we go people acknowledge us.

"Walk tall brother, you got a queen there."

"Take care of that sister brer."

"Soul sister."

"Get on with your bad self."

Feel the hump in my back go as I straighten to be worthy of this queen. It's something new, a respect they have for self and kind that didn't exist three, four years ago. The fire and rebellions have drawn them closer. Blinking into Lenox, feel night closing. On '15th Street, she sees the crowds from the snake pit.

"What's happening over there? Must be an accident?"

'15th and Lenox is the mouth of a sewer where the junkies from the block wash up. A play street kept from traffic by wooden barriers at either end. In summer till late night crowded with people. Kids playing. Dope dealers occupy the halls and stoops surrounded by lookouts, lieutenants and customers. Crap game against the curb holds the sports, two white cops on the corner. If you stand here ten minutes, someone you once knew and wondered what had happened to will come by.

"No accident, like this all the time, all these people standing round are junkies."

A young kid comes strolling by, bout twelve years old in a black beaver hat, bright colored knit, matching silk pants and alligator shoes, counting a wad of money, unafraid as his little partners watch his back. He sings his sale. "I got it, the smoker, my bag killed Frankie Lyman last week."

Nandy looks at him disbelieving as he joins the crap game of old men.

The streets are alive with children and death around the edges where junkies stalk and nod. Black faces everywhere move and press against me, filling me with energy. This place breeds strange men. They go mad and are unable to exist outside its bounds without constant transfusions.

"Look at that sign." She points to a restaurant window. In bright red letters: NO DOPE PEDALING ALLOWED. "All these people are addicts? But there are hundreds of them!"

Whenever we approach they draw away, not wanting to soil her with their touch. Crossing '16th she stops to read billboards on a burnt out building advertising dances and shows. Another sign catches our eye: MUGGERS, RAPISTS AND THIEVES BEWARE, WE ARE ARMED AND GOING TO KILL YOU. WE THE CITIZENS OF HARLEM ARE TIRED OF YOU PREYING UPON US. BEWARE WE MEAN BUSINESS.

"Hey Cain." A stranger slides out the shadows, hugs me and becomes cousin Jimmy.

"Hey man, how you been? Nandy, this my cousin Jimmy."

"When'd you raise, looking good. Still messing around? I'm doing something."

"What you got?"

"Deuces."

"Got some place I can get off?"

"Yeah, we go by the house. Mom be glad to see you."

"How she doing?"

"Okay, just come out the hospital last week."

We come to Manhattan Avenue. Remember the building from childhood, high ceilinged lobby and elevator, now half burned and filthy. Jimmy opens the door, signals silence and tips through the hall.

"Jimmy that you?" He straightens like a caught thief.

"Look who I found Mom."

Aunt A sits in front the TV staring till recognition comes. "God damn. George Jr. and who is this you've got with you?" Kissing me, she steps back.

"Aunt A, this is Nandy, a friend."

"You know girl haven't seen this nephew of mine in years. Boy what you been doing with yourself. Sit down and tell me something. Want a drink? Don't drink? Good, bad for you." She pulls a bottle from under her pillow and pours herself a shot. Jimmy calls from the back room and I leave them talking.

"What you say you wanted?"

"Couple of bags."

Start to get off, the blood shows and clots. I squeeze the bulb and stuff flies all over the place. Hear Aunt A's footsteps and snatch the apparatus from my arm and drop it behind the bed. Jimmy pains as he wipes up the precious liquid.

"What you two doing back here? Come on out front, don't trust you sitting back here with Jimmy."

Sit a few minutes while she carries on bout my childhood.

"Aunt A, sorry we can't stay longer but we've got to get back."

"Okay son, it's good to see you again. Take care of this girl, she's better than you deserve and don't stay away so long, your old aunt ain't got much longer in this world. But do stay away from your cousin Jimmy cause he ain't never up to no good. What was he trying to get you to do back there? Okay George, give the family my love."

Jimmy joins us downstairs. "Which way you going? Uptown? I got to get back to the bar and take care of business. Whenever you get ready you can find me there. If not, I'm home. Nice meeting you sister. Later George."

"Your aunt's something else. I like her. What were you and Jimmy talking about before, couldn't understand a word?"

"Dope, he wanted to know if I was still using stuff."

Walk down '16th and eat dinner in a Spanish restaurant. On the way back to the hotel start coming down. The world goes in stop time, but I decide to go to the Playhouse anyway. Want to hear the music of the dream before I wake. Jazz. Live and loud. One of them young monsters blowing. City-bred nigger. Sounds like he heard the tongue spoken by Trane's terrible voice. He cooks, the place is smoke-filled and garish.

"Jazz is the city. Only city niggers can feel this thing. I never liked it much, never listened really, hadn't been here long enough. To my country ear it was mad noise. But I'm a part of the tremendous pressure that generates that sound and I feel it so good now."

This woman is mine, hear her as she leads me in the discovery of myself while the breakdown begins. Feel myself outside myself as we follow the music, shattered into a million tiny fragments chasing the sound, all outside ourselves, traveling a vastness together as we try to save my soul. Step lively nigger, stop lagging. The music talks of Babylon, bedlam, 110th on up. Them killing streets where the heat and garbage in summer kill you, where cold eats your ass in winter, when dying is every minute. Oh, the pain, it's terrible, want to scream, feel the spirit, whole, and come out of myself. Her pressure returns me. I hear the music again, it talks of the sixties, the rebellion, excitement, broken glass and bullets flying. Was in prison during these years and now experience my period of absence. Read newspaper and factual accounts of the events, but they're distorted to meet and suit the needs of the majority, now I'm hearing and feeling that time as it truly happened. Jazz is history. Listening, can hear and feel the development of the people. Can hear the new-found respect that I didn't understand in the streets, its origins, all in the music.

The musician, his purpose and role are understood. They denied us a tongue and we fashioned our own in which we told and recorded the unwritten history of our stay in Babylon. The set ends and I'm getting sicker so we head in.

Am afraid to sleep with Nandy, make love to her. Been so long since I've made love to a woman without my medicine, don't think I can. And to a sister? Have been with only white women where I enjoyed the advantage of the myths each of us brought to bed. Joanie was had in a narcotic stupor. Have never come to a woman naked and defenseless, just a man. Am shamed knowing I know nothing of black women.

This shall be the last time sleep will come easy for a while, have to get to bed. Undress quickly and put the light out. She lies beside me and I begin a discourse on my inability to have sex while kicking, how my nervous system in disintegration will not respond or react properly—afraid of the passion locked in her dark body. She feels me and I tremble.

"What you shaking for, chills?"

She drapes herself around me, warming my soul. Ache with desire and squeeze her, trying to liberate myself. Feel the flesh hindering us till we find a rhythm. Her body and hot mouth, there's nothing else. Her fingers move over face and body eliciting sensations delightful from a dead man. Feel it filling me to the exclusion of all else warm and alive, passion, need, resurrecting me. Tear at each other sinking into love, talking crazy sounds, love's language. Till we've escaped and travel the vastness together again. The flesh is only the means to an end not the end itself. Another device to get outside yourself and be One. Squeeze her wanting to merge our bodies and suddenly the elusive soul is free.

V

GEORGIE IS A FAGGOT, teacher's pet!"

"Fight, fight!"

"Hit him one good!"

"Here comes Reverend McKenzie, break it up!"

"Here, here, break this up. Now what's this all about?"

"He started it Sir."

"That true George?"

"He called me names."

"Now that's silly, names can't hurt you and you young man shouldn't go around calling people names. Now shake hands and let's not have any more of this. Want to talk with you George, walk with me. Hear we're going to lose you, you're going to move soon. How do you feel about it?"

"Don't wanna move, was born here, all my friends and everything are here."

"You're young George, but when you're older, you'll understand what I'm going to tell you. You're different from the other boys, Willy, Joe and the rest. God gave you more than them and it's up to you and your parents to take advantage of His gift.

They're doing the right thing by moving out of this place. They realize that you were meant for better things that you could never receive here. They're doing this for you. It's a great sacrifice but someday you'll repay them. Tell your Nana, was by the hospital to see your mother. Bye George."

"THAT YOU GEORGE?"

"Yes Nana."

"Give me a kiss and go wash. Dinner's almost ready and your father be home in a minute. Lord what happened to you?"

"I had a fight."

"Here, let me clean your face, you've got an ugly scratch on your head. Hold still now, this is going to hurt a little. There, didn't bat an eye, aren't we strong. Flo? That you? Come here take a look at George, he had a fight in school."

"Oh Mother, there's nothing wrong with him, it's only a scratch, he's too big to get hurt. Did you win? Who was it? Willy Smith, hope you gave it to him good."

"Now Flo, stop talking like that. Don't want no grandson of mine out there fighting in the streets like riffraff."

"Oh Mother he's only a child and his father did it often enough."

"Nana, why do we have to move and leave you and Auntie Flo. What'll I do?"

"Come on now, you're a big boy. It's not that bad. Of course we'll miss you, but we'll see each other and you'll spend weekends here. Don't you worry."

"George, your mother had a baby boy. You're a big brother now. What happened to you? Really now, fighting in school, you should know better, how many times have I told you. Did you win? Watch, you lead with your left. Jab, jab, hook, that's it. Try it again."

Long into the night we talked of father and son things.

"You're getting big now, you're number two man in the house. You got a baby brother to take care of. I may not always be here and it'll be up to you to take care of Mom.

"We're moving to get you away from here son, this is a slum.

"You're born with two strikes against you son and the third pitch is coming right down the middle and you've got to be ready for it. Ride it out of sight. By moving we're helping to get you ready, prepare you for what's out there. I'm telling you these things not to scare you, but to make it easier for you when you're older. See, I had no one to tell me and it comes like a shock. One more thing before you go to bed, be better than best at anything you do."

Sleep a happy sleep child.

MOVING WAS MADNESS, nothing but ill winds blowing no good. Our arrival greeted by a blizzard, white filling the eye, falling day and night, confining me to the hostile house, trapped for days in the strange place. Always crying. Wondering why we'd left the old home. Didn't go to school cause we weren't going to be here long. The houses were only quonset huts, temporary shelters till the returning G.I.'s found homes.

Only companion a winding muddy river, coming from where I didn't know but flowing nowhere fast. It moved sluggishly under the bridge where cars went, fragrant with mild-smelling garbage. Sitting on the bank throwing stones, watched them vanish into ripples. Walked on it when frozen feeling the movement beneath my feet, infecting me with its restlessness. They came to play on the other side, hated them for violating my privacy, for doing as I did. I hated them for their camaraderie. Every day they came, animated, noisy, every day they saw me sitting, frozen as the ice, looking from green eyes, looking down from loneliness, longing for their friendship. One day they called me. Couldn't hear over the distance, but smiled and waved thinking they were greeting me. They waved back but I still couldn't hear. Smiled and waved again, they pointed at me and laughed and I laughed with joy, wanting to cross the river and join them. Heard the rocks' dull thudding in the soft mud, could see them still laughing, yelling, young faces distorted. Unfeeling the rocks striking me, no fear, confusion, couldn't understand. Hit in the forehead, blood blinded my eyes, tumbled down and turned the ground red. There was no pain but I screamed feeling the warm blood, tasting it, could hear them calling, fainter, was running. Covered with blood ran through the streets eluding strangers asking crazy questions. Mom screamed and hugging me washed the blood and hurt away. She couldn't understand why somebody would want to hurt somebody else. Never went back to the river, fascination was gone.

How long did I live there? Couldn't have been long. Another image presents itself. Another place but close in time for it's gilded in the same gold ever-awakening light, when all things were new impressing themselves indelibly on consciousness. Walking in a huge sprawling complex of brick red buildings. Towering in the ever-present sunlight, threatening in their silence. High-rising façade, curtained windows. What passed in the cells of solitude? The place was different with its abundant and in-turned love, a little like Harlem. Children uprooted from former hovels and placed here without rhyme or reason. We ran the new streets seeking and making friends. First day there I met C.J., he stood around and watched us move in.

Nandy's arm bracelets ring as she moves from bed. Watch her wrapped in a blanket wash the sleep from her eyes.

"Morning lover."

"Morning yourself. How you feel?"

"Love you woman of mine."

"Love you man. How do you feel?"

"Good, oh so good, come here." We wrestle and play around laughing.

"You don't act like a sick man."

"Give it time. Let's go eat while I still can."

Wash and go down. Pick up a paper and order breakfast while she phones home and the job. Go through the paper carefully, page by page and there's no mention of a rape. J.B.'s right. She probably won't say anything. Wonder what Bu's told Nichole, does she know or understand what she saw? It's starting, feel the slight headache, pain in the back and bowels churning. Through the window see a dope transaction going down and without thinking, out of habit, I run outside to cop.

"Give me three."

"Three what? What you talking about? Don't know you, get away from me."

The dealer hurries down the street looking over his shoulder to see if I'm following and I go back inside. Should've known he'd nut on me. I don't even look like a junky.

"Everything's okay. Told them I'd be out for a few days and Mom'll take care of Tchaka. How you feeling?"

"Starting to really come down."

The attempt and near success of scoring aggravates the illness. It's like that. You can be sick, but not until you cop or have the money to cop do you really come down. My nose and eyes start running, stuff yawns and stomach talking. Fill up on liquids hoping to ease the stomach cramps I know are coming. Back in the room fall on the bed while Nandy watches me and reads the paper.

WE'D MOVED FROM NANA'S and it was one of my weekend visits. Coming from sleep, so early it was, the red sun warmed me under the quilt. It was Saturday and the house was quiet, Granny, Nana and Auntie Flo sleeping. Throwing off the blankets and feeling the morning air, I was still, enjoying the delicious sensation of waking. It was a grand bed, the one my mother and father had slept in. Had a headboard full of compartments, with a radio and the comic books I'd fallen asleep over the night before. Turned on the radio and waited forever till it warmed up. Read the comics, impatient for the house to wake. Finished reading and tired of music, was hungry and wanted breakfast. Tipped through the house, hesitating outside Granny's room listening for her snore, then into the bathroom to wash and back to my room.

Looking out the window I forgot hunger. Tops of buildings were covered in a warm light showing carved cornices of acanthus, papyrus leaves, lions and gargoyles. Pigeons had whitened parts of buildings with waste and cooed softly just waking. Preening themselves, showed iridescent purple green colored breasts. Testing early morning wings they flew short stuttering flights returning to perch. The sky was glorious blue and the bird man was on the roof across the way leading his charges. All I could see of him was the brown stick he urged and shooed his birds from the coop with into the blue. Follow the leader, they made circles in the sky, lost from view and returning again.

Windows were still closed against the chill night air and curtained from inquisitive eyes. Flaking fire escapes, rusted orange and black were pretty in the morning with green and red flowers set out. Nana had hers in the window and I would turn the soil and water them. A window goes up across the way and Bootsy waves, wanting to know if I'm going to play stickball, then disappears.

The bottom of the canyon, stoops, streets and stores were still in shadows, no people or cars. Then the junkman's cry broke the stillness and seemed a sign for the world to wake. Windows were thrown up, dust mops and rags shaken out into the backyards and clotheslines drawn in. Smelled breakfasts cooking, all kinds of good things reviving hunger and heard Nana moving in the kitchen.

"Raaaaags ol Irn." The junkman came upstreet slowly singing. Brown horse and green wagon, tired and old, ringing bell and horse's hooves clip-clopping in the quiet. People set out stacks of newspaper, rags, scrap metal, mattresses and springs by the curb and returned to breakfast. Nana sometimes let me take things down and I'd wait for him to help load and rummage in the garbage. Smell of the horse, riding in the seat with Mr. Charles. Hearing him talk to his horse, Tomorrow, in that funny way, "gee" and "haw." I'd hold the reins and feel the life at my fingertips as Mr. Charles took a long swallow of his medicine. Clip, clop, squeaking wheels, bell ringing, a cry of rags old iron.

Turning from the window, I went quietly to the kitchen, Auntie Flo and Granny were still sleeping. Pancakes and sausage smelled good, and Nana in floured apron stood over the fires. Took the spatula and watched them while she went to the icebox. The popping grease burned and I'd duck and laugh trying to turn the cakes. We ate together, she saying grace, always so rapidly, I'd never learned it. Only snatches when she or my father had slowed to catch their breath and ending, "Christ redeem His sake amen." While we were eating, Auntie Flo came and poured her coffee. She couldn't eat or talk till she had her coffee and smoked a cigarette. If I bothered her enough she'd give me a cup, all milk and sugar. Finished, I'd help dry the dishes and make the beds before going down, promising to stay in sight.

Raced down the five flights at breakneck and exited into morning. The iceman was coming up the street. We kids crowded around watching the crusher, catching and sucking on the flying chips. Those common chips of ice tasted so good. Bootsy came down with a stick and ball and we sat on the stoop waiting for the gang.

The streets begin filling, women wheeling carts and children off to market. Men passing a bottle and talking. Watch them in their bright mismatched colored clothes. Bright colors. Can tell they're from a tropic place, jungle colors you never saw downtown, reds, yellows, greens, bright bird plumage. Feel it all inside me. The scene's beauty composed of mismatch, unarranged and ever-changing, without intention, design, dependent precisely upon the accidental blending of unharmonious elements.

When the gang shows, Ziggy, Jeter, Blue, Ugmo, Tank and the rest, we choose sides. Playing in the middle of the street and halting traffic till a play was over. Drivers escaping the block muttered and cursed us, we laughed and cursed back. This was our street, most of us had been born on it, we and the concrete were so intimate, the streets were an extension of the house. It was the passerby who was trespassing on our property, not the other way around.

See the ball rising black out of the canyon's shade, soaring above the buildings into light, pink against blue. Following its flight with my eyes, legs pumping madly, see it fall, lost for a moment returning to shadows, bounding off a building, a fire escape, rolling off and again in space, then caught for an out. The sidewalks and stoops are crowded with men who watch and applaud, recalling themselves in some far off time engaged in similar sport. Remember the happy times, but even then there was the tension that could be set off any moment.

The car didn't stop in time and knocked Blue down. People came off stoops, out of buildings, bars and stupors. Women screamed, his mother fell and cried over him, his sisters and neighbors wailed hysterical, some prayed and Blue bled. They dragged the driver from the car, beating him bloody. The tension and anger that lay in the air and people exploded. Words I'd never uttered but heard shouted all round me went in my ears and out my mouth. Charged and screaming, "Kill the bastard!" They tried to hang the unconscious body from a lamppost, but no one could find a rope. Police and ambulance rescued him.

He was white but that had nothing to do with it, or maybe it had all to do with it. Not knowing the law of the land he was traveling. He'd honked and honked arrogantly for us to move out his way and we stalled and stalled. Didn't he know it was our street? That he was on our time not his? If he'd known, he'd never have hit Blue cause he'd driven different, waited.

The people hooted and jeered, throwing things from windows. Order was restored with the arrival of more police. They left, sirens screaming, and we began to destroy the car till someone set it afire, making a charred memorial to Blue and misunderstanding.

NANA CALLED ME FROM PLAY to get ready and go shopping. Held our fare in a dirty hand as she boarded the bus and found seats, then stood watching the change fall in the glass box, ringing as it struck the glass and metal. The driver turned a handle and the change disappeared, reappearing from a chute on the side where he caught it and placed it in the correct slots of his coin-changer. Was amazed by his skill, the entire operation was done blind, without fault while his eyes and other hand drove the big bus.

Sitting by the window watched the streets pass, changing black to white. The hurrying people in all their mystery. Wondered what went on in every street and where they were going. We passed through my neighborhood, saw the projects, people I knew and wanted to call them, but knew better. When we passed the house, we'd smile, not having to wonder what went on behind the walls or who the people were. Wanted to stand up and announce, like they did in the sightseeing bus on the class trip, that this was where I lived. See the window with the blue curtains? That's my room and next to it the living room. There's my school, wanted to acquaint them with my life so they'd not have to wonder and feel strange like me when passing different places.

As we neared downtown, the scene became more commercial, fruit stalls, shops. Streets crowded with people. Bags and carts overflowing with goods. Riding the bus and separated from it all by a pane of glass was nothing. But when you got off the pandemonium overwhelmed you and you felt its magnificence. Nana held me while people bumped and jostled us, leading slowly through holes in the crowd, stopping here, there, comparing prices, arguing, bargaining.

The noise was deafening, so many sounds. Honking traffic, stopping, starting, piercing police whistles controlling its flow. Crackling trashcan fires eating wooden crates, old Christmas trees showering heat and sparks down on you. Vendors beside their shined pyramids of fruit and vegetables, hawking em loud, "Red matoes, tatoes, nannas." So many colors threatening blindness. People, black, white, yellow. Yellow buses, green cabs.

"Red matoes, white tatoes, yellow nannas." European accents distorting these common words gave them a freshness. All color cars and checker cabs, red dime store, hotdog stand, stacks and rows of gay colored fruits, shined and freshly wet. White aprons and bright plaid shirts the vendors' uniform. Bold colored signs selling bargains.

Air smelling of fruits and vegetables, burning wood and gasoline fumes. So many good things to eat, hotdog men calling out, "Redhots!" Strange sights to see, a novelty salesman with mechanical toys that strutted boldly under trampling feet. Men in bloodstained aprons pushed open meat wagons hung with carcasses, yelling, "Watch it, watch it! Hot stuff, hot stuff!"

Young boys and old people selling shopping bags, "Shopping bags, shopping bags, shopping bag Miss, five cent shopping bags." Selling one they'd knock it open with a bang and flourish. The silent blind man selling pencils in the front dime store with his Seeing Eye dog. A hundred conversations in as many languages, mingling and sounding the same.

All this occurred simultaneously, crashing and overwhelming the senses. I'd arrive at the butcher shop, a distance of half a block from the bus stop, breathless and tired.

It was cool inside and the closed door shut out the street noise. A barnlike place with rails running through the air on which rolled carcasses. Painted cold and white, floor covered with saw-dust to catch the dripping blood that spotted everything, aprons, glass, cabinets. It was noisy with men moving about taking orders, slamming freezers, registers ringing and dull-thudding axes on the block.

Louie was our butcher and while he filled our order I'd watch him through the glass seeing only a bloody apron moving back and forth. Finally he'd reach over the counter and hand me a hunk of salted bologna which I'd share with Nana, she'd remind me to thank him since I never seemed to remember and they'd smile at this private joke enacted so many times. I'd never really forget. It was only to enjoy their smiles and attention that I pretended to. He called me Junior, having known my father and as I grew he'd comment how he'd seen me grow from nothing and I'd think how I'd seen him grow old before my eyes.

One section of the shop lured me, the icebox. Only caught glimpses of the interior when the butchers went in or out for cuts of meat. Red blood and raw meat against the white curling clouds of vapor sent the mind on grotesque fancies. Locked in there at night and being found frozen and hanging with the cows next morning.

With our order filled and bill tallied we'd go to the cashier. A glass booth with a porthole through which you spoke and paid money. She was a pretty lady with gold hair, reminding me of fairy tales and captive maidens. Smiling she'd give me a piece of candy and ask about the family. I'd remember to thank her. Getting her change, Nana'd wrap a tip in the receipt and standing tiptoe I'd hand it to Louie.

When it was almost noon, we'd leave our packages to go eat lunch and finish shopping. We ate what Nana called our running lunch, stopping at a hotdog stand or pizza place, maybe the dime store for hamburgers and malts, usually eating as we walked. Dessert came from the fruit purchases, pulling oranges, apples, pears or plums from a bag.

There was a notions shop we visited every week. A small store stuck between vegetable stands. Dim-lit place crammed with articles, bundles of gay colored cloth, buttons, needles, spools of thread and catalogues of women's dress patterns that Nana pored over with childish delight. While she was engrossed, I'd wait outside on the crowded street warming myself by the burning trashcan. Boys selling shopping bags hung around its warmth talking about money and ways of making it, each telling how much he'd made, jingling the coins in his pockets. Sometimes they'd be pitching pennies, and though I knew Nana wouldn't approve I tossed once then quit. They got mad, told em they could have the money back but they refused it. When Nana came out and we walked away could feel their eyes burning my back. Finished shopping returned to Louie's for the meat and made the long walk to the bus stop. She'd carry the meat since it was heavy and I the fruit and other things. How many times had the heavy packages almost slipped from my tired arms but drawing strength from somewhere I'd make it. The sun was down then, the crowds gone and trashcans extinguished. Tired and full, fell asleep, waking when Nana hunched me and we were home.

A LUMP STICKS IN MY THROAT, can't breathe or swallow. Gagging, run to the toilet and vomit. Live things, frogs and insects kick in the liquid coming out. The empty stomach dry heaves like it's coming inside out, ups juices and yellow bile, knocks me to my knees with pain.

"Nandy, water, get water!"

Down it and bring it right up. The cramps subside and she helps me off the floor. In bed I burn and freeze. Have never kicked cold in the streets, always in jails where there wasn't any dope. There mind and body protected me against the intense pain by rejecting pain. But out here, pockets full of money and dope in the streets, everything is intensified, screaming for relief. The walls close, inanimate objects turn on me and colors leap from objects to tell of themselves. My eyes are affected with magnification, see the most minute things in great detail. Pebbled texture of walls, great canyons and valleys in the nappy blanket, pores in Nandy's skin. I'm gone mad in frenzy.

The pain begins. Comes softly first, touching me lightly and increasing in intensity and frequency till I'm all pain. There is no pause. Each stroke prepares me for the next which is even harder till the screaming crescendo. It lasts three days. Sweat pops off me and freezes. I chatter, can't talk. Nandy frightened feels my head and pulse.

"Baby let me call a doctor. You can't do it this way, you'll kill yourself. There's one in the hotel, I'll call down."

"A doctor won't help."

"Let me try George. Can't see you hurt like this."

Tears run and I feel myself coming apart. She calls the desk and gets the doctor's office. Stagger into the elevator barely able to stand, so weak and tired. Want a fix. Can't kick this way. In the office the receptionist takes my name. Finally he calls us in.

"And what's your problem?"

Seeing Nandy with me and our hesitancy—"What's wrong with you young people? If you're going to do these things, you should be prepared. There's just no excuse for it in this day and age. You, young lady are just as responsible as he, they have all sorts of contraceptive devices, and you sir, you're old enough to know better. Who recommended you to me? I don't perform such operations, but I'll give you a number to call. They'll take care of you. . . ."

I don't understand, then realize. "No, that's not our problem, doctor."

"What is your problem then?"

"I'm a drug addict."

He backs up from the desk like I was coming across it and draws a pistol.

"Well?"

"I'm a drug addict and I need help."

"Can't do anything for you."

"You can't do anything for him? He's sick, in pain. He's a sick man, you're a doctor. What do you mean you can't do anything for him?"

"Exactly what I said. I can't do anything for him."

"Why? Why can't you? He's sick. Look at him. You can give him something for the pain. You're a doctor. He's got chills, a fever."

"Get out of my office before I call the police. There are other patients out front I have to see."

"Look doctor, I'm sick, in pain like anybody else that comes to you."

"Told you to get out of here."

"Come on Nandy."

"He wouldn't help you. You're sick, he's a doctor and he wouldn't help you. Why baby? Why? What's wrong with these people? They're crazy. When you get well, we're getting out of here. Going to get away from this place. You'll come home with me. It's different down there baby. There's no dope. No madness like up here. You can raise children, not always wondering what they're doing, what's happening to them. Oh baby couldn't live here worrying about you, every time you stepped outdoors and weren't right back. Wondering if the police got you, are you dead of an O.D. He wouldn't help us baby. Why? They must want you this way. That's it. They want you sick, stealing and robbing, acting like you crazy. They must cause otherwise they'd do something about it. Want something to eat?"

"Can't eat, water, that's all."

Feel my body fighting, eliminating the poison, pissing and sweating. Smell the heroin, like metal. Pain in the back, muscles and nerves jumping. Roil around like in a fit. A demon jumps out my head. It is the only way to fight this thing, like it's alive and two-legged. Lay hands on it and throw it off my back. Cannot sit still and let nature take its course. Must take positive action, confront this thing trying to steal my soul. Can't believe in red blood cells, white blood cells, in any clinical analyses of detoxification. Must believe that I'm fighting for my life against a real life foe who's standing over me, waiting to claim me. There is no sleep, but occasionally exhaustion steals me, and I dream and remember.

"NAME?"

"George Cain."

"Since you're so tall George, I'll have to seat you in the rear. The other children couldn't see over you."

Laughter. Derisive children's laughter.

"The only student to score a perfect exam was George Cain."

"George is a faggot, teacher's pet."

Always fighting, coming home beaten, always running.

"Look son you've got to stop letting these kids pick on you. You're bigger than they are, why do you let them pick on you? What are you afraid of? You don't like to fight? What kind of answer is that? You want a beating every day? Well every time you lose one and come running in here like you're crazy, I'm going to give you one. Now take this pillow and practice. Left, right. Harder, harder, that's it. Every day you're going to practice and I don't want you coming home whining about somebody chasing you, otherwise I'll give it to you and good."

"George, not again! These children, why don't they leave you alone? That's okay son we love you. No, I won't tell your father."

The fights were just as frequent but I began winning. They banded together then, jeering and taunting, to chase me home. One day they cornered me in the schoolyard, there was no place to run. Their leader, a redheaded kid, walked up. Saw their faces blur and merge to one waiting for me to plead, cry, anything. Fear took me and I hit him, again and again, afraid if I stopped he'd hit me. He fell and I kicked him until pulled off screaming and crying.

"You're probably wondering why I sent for you. No, it's nothing too serious, not yet at least. Does your son talk to you? About what goes on in school? Then you do know he had a fight yesterday? And that he's had many others? He's told you about them? Well he had a fight with another student, the boy had to be taken to the hospital where he's in serious condition. We're running a school not a boxing arena. I know he's an excellent student. One of our best as a matter of fact and his behavior in class is exemplary, but reports have reached me that he's rebellious, difficult to approach, causes disharmony among the other students, on the whole quite unmanageable. No, no, he hasn't said or done anything, it's just his attitude. What's wrong with him? No friends, doesn't seem to want any, not at all normal and yet he's one of our brightest students. I was wondering if you could shed any light on the problem, after all you are his parents. Nothing, no ideas? Well you see he's so much bigger than the other children and this last incident only points out what I've said. It must stop before he really hurts someone. You'll speak to him then. Very good. Was nice meeting and talking with you."

"What happened with that fight you had yesterday? What do you mean you just had a fight, don't know. Didn't raise you to be no boxer, do you know that boy's in the hospital, you're only a kid and already you're maiming people, Lord help us when you get bigger. You're too big to go around picking on people, you're going to hurt someone bad one day. Don't tell me they pick on you, no George, not as big as you are. Don't tell me that and don't tell me what I said before. I'm telling you now, if I ever hear tell of you fighting again, you're going to get it. Stop telling me what I said before. Stop that crying. Said stop it, before I give you something to cry about.

"Now what's this they tell me about no friends? How do you expect to have any if you go around picking on people? You know what you are? A bully and nobody likes a bully. You don't like them. Well you better learn to and fast. I don't want to hear any more about it. Now get out of here. I've got work to do. Remember what I said and stop that sniveling."

"Go ahead, cry son, it's going to be all right. Your father's angry. When people are angry, they say things they don't mean. Of course he loves you, whatever made you think he didn't? He's got so many things on his mind. He's getting ready to graduate, someday you'll go to college and see what it's like. Feel better? Drink your tea. Do Mother a favor? All I want you to do is try. No more fighting and try to make friends. They don't understand you, that's why it's so hard, but you'll try, for me? I just got an idea, how would you like to join the Y? They've lots of things for boys to do. Swimming, trips, sports, all kinds of things, new people to meet. You could make friends there. How's that sound? You like that? I'll talk to your father and see what he says."

THE Y WAS UP THE STREET from the projects. We sat in the office dressed in Sunday waiting to see the director, a white-haired man, twinkle in eye and gold in his mouth. He shook my hand, asked a lot of questions, accepted the twelve dollar yearly fee and told me to return the next day. We met in his office for a tour of the building, me and five others who'd joined that week. He spoke with us briefly.

"You'll see some odd things and people, but we at the Y feel you're grown enough to respect this. That's one of our purposes here, to teach respect for all men. To instill in you the principles of our founder and organization, to make you whole in body, mind and spirit. In short, to make you men fit to rule the world of tomorrow."

Our first stop was the pool. Looking down on the green chlorined water and pretty tiles, couldn't wait to swim till I saw the naked men splashing and floating around.

"They're naked. How come they ain't got nothing on? Don't wanna swim naked. I got a bathing suit."

"It's our policy that swimming this way engenders in you a healthy respect for the grace and beauty of the human body. Look at those men, how healthy they are. Beautiful, beautiful."

The kid behind me whispered in my ear and pointed, "Look at that, will ya. Look at the balls on that guy." The pool was like an echo chamber and everybody heard him just as clear. This guy had a hernia and his balls, like hairy coconuts, hung down around his knees. We stared agape and cracked up.

In the gym an exercise class was in progress. Tired old men tried to keep pace with a young instructor who counted so fast he was killing them. They coughed, wheezed, spat up and seemed determined to die that way. Above the gym, a bank track with antique figures plodding methodically in circles till they could go no more. The place stank of old age and funky sneakers.

Another room was full of gymnasts. Men swinging from loops, spinning through the air and flipping on trampolines. There was a weightlifting area. Here they were, those beautiful bodies, powerful and massive from lifting weights. Snatching, jerking, lifting. Pictured myself someday like them. There was something wrong, I didn't know what it was. The way the perfect bodies sat in a trance before the mirrors struck dumb by their own image, staring at themselves staring back and flexing their muscles. Or was it the way they walked so delicately, with mincing steps like they'd fall and break.

The tour over, he left us in a room while he went to find our group leader and I met my new friends. Jose, James and Bushy. Seemed every black mother with a misfit child had enrolled him in the Y that week. We were all too tall, too big, too smart or too something where we couldn't work or play well with others in school. While we stood around laughing about the guy in the pool, this young guy came in.

"Guess you know each other. My name's Bill, plain Bill, no Mister. You got that? I'm your group leader. Want us to be friends. I'm going to get you guys in shape, make you the toughest outfit in this joint, not like these sissies and snot noses they got running round here."

Getting in shape began with rigorous daily exercises. He'd

been a top kick during the war and we drilled and exercised like crazy—"to weld you into a formidable unit and instill discipline."

Hours on end, half-stepping, double time, rear marching, lefting, righting. Across the street in the park we practiced commando tactics. Sneaking up on trees, rocks and hidden lovers. Lord we were ready for war. The other kids in the Y hated us. We were so big and getting bigger, twelve years old and almost six feet tall, filled with pride and arrogance. We were strong, a unit, no longer lonely kids needing love. The magic this man worked on our young minds. We bought Army jackets and jump boots and strutted boldly around in stern dignity like young S.S. Seeing this change, my people thought it newfound confidence.

"I'm proud of you, you're the best bunch of men I've ever seen."

To Bill, we were men and this was the key to his success. But it was in the clubroom where Bill practiced his most potent medicine. Long dissertations on sex, broads and the great war. Perpetuating his hates in our new minds. He showed us scenes of Army life and French flicks on a slide projector. His commentaries on women were brief, "Bitches, all they're good for is fucking."

One day Jose and me were in the boxing room, there was this funny smell and this old guy said to us, "You kids wanna see something funny?" and pulling down his shorts showed an erection. Scared we ran and got Bill and the gang. We hunted the guy down, finally cornering him on the staircase. Bill knocked him down and like lion cubs we joined in the kill, kicking and beating him senseless.

"One thing I can't stand's a cocksucker, kill every last one of the bastards."

This thought spoken so often and vehemently became part of us. Of all our diversions, witch hunting was the most noble, for here we had a right and were doing the world a service. What else had fags been born for? To beat on and steal from. The row-boat lake and fountain were the hunting grounds, cause there was where they made advances to us from the boats. Me and Jose'd stand by the water since we were the tallest and the others hid in the bushes or on the island.

"Hey baby, you know how to row a boat?"

Two gaily dressed men rowed over and invited us aboard. When close enough we'd all pile in, singing noisily and pulling hard on the oars, heading for the deserted island.

Apprehensive, but unable to do anything, they waited joyfully for the rape they'd dreamed of so often, or the terrible beating. To them it didn't make any difference, they'd tell envying friends of the horrible pain and how many stitches it took to repair the damage. "My dear, it still hurts some."

Or they'd lie around for days recovering, telling friends of the trials their so sensitive souls had been put through by some jealous lover. Even with our knives at their throats they'd move about so to rest their bodies against ours and feel us with their touch.

The island was in the middle of the lake. We forced them from the boat to a hidden wood and made them strip. Took all their valuables and beat them till we saw a boat heading our way. Next day page 2 of the *News* read: PIRACY ON CENTRAL PARK LAKE.

In broad daylight five young thugs attacked and beat two young men on Central Park Lake. In true Jolly Roger fashion, they rowed the men to a deserted island where they forced them to walk the plank, then beat and robbed them. The two are in good condition at Roosevelt Hospital. Police are looking for suspects.

BILL WENT ON VACATION and the group disbanded for summer. Began drinking then to kill the long summer days

with nothing to do. For a few cents winos would buy you all
the pluck wanted. Hid under the highway by the river. Sitting
on the rotten pier swayed by the gently slapping water, the lights
of Jersey reflected on the blackness like party lights. Boats bass-
tooted, distant and lonely. My mind following them beyond the
harbor. The loud screech of trains in the yard behind me, rubber
wheels slapping on the highway above. All that movement of men
and things had infected me and I dreamt of long trips and foreign
places. Was young then, still possessed child's vision, everything
was beautiful and unquestionable.

Swilled hardily and the liquor settled a hot ball in the stomach,
warming me all over. Watched the dirty river, oil slicks colored
rainbow, old rubbers, dead rats floating upside down, wood, dead
fish with white bellies. Use to swim here, me, Smitty, Tommy.
Tommy drowned out there, head caught in a floating milk can.
They dredged him up days later fish eaten and water blown. Barges
moved slowly upriver high-piled with garbage, bits spilled into the
water and hungry fish fooled rose to feed, struggling, shone all
colors in the sun then vanished into gull's beak. After a while the
barges be specks passing under the bridge.

She walks to the river's edge, moving gracefully feminine. She
is woman. Turning, she spots me and I look friendly. Drawn, she
comes and sits down. "I'm Carla, felt you calling me and I came."

She's beautiful, more than woman, sounds like a bitch, gestures, manner, perfectly feminine. Not awkward absurd like a
faggot, some gross parody. Is woman, why wasn't she born so.

"I'm sorry, I'll go."

"I'm Cain."

The words leave me, neither asking or demanding, but final
and past as if her staying is already done.

Am drunk and talking crazy, words from some part of self I

don't know. Her hand is soft, like a woman's, and crazy things go
on in my head.

"You're beautiful."

"You're beautiful, more than woman. Why weren't you born
one. No that's not what I mean, cause then you wouldn't be you.
You're too beautiful to be."

She's still delighting in my touch, hearing long ago dreamt
things she'd always hoped to hear.

Talking drunk and far away—"Your mother should've killed
you when you were born, smothered you under a pillow. This
world can only kill you."

Kiss her, kill her, pretty boy girl. Break the bottle, watch her,
know it must be done. Hurry, hurry, do it. Rising in me, like in
church, growing assuming form, love warm and yellow colored.
Struggling, not wanting to yield. Then it's on me, painful, bringing tears, bursting with its warmth. Unuttered the thought leaves
me and covers us in grace. I feed the glass to the river. Her fingers
move over my face, feeling in my stomach. Can't turn from her
green eyes, no desire to push away, only the strange anticipation
preceding the unknown. Her face comes near, life's breath on my
face, lips touching. Gone, gone as if it never were and I jump back
angry and deadly, feeling a fool. For an instant, glimpsed beatific,
gone and only a vacancy out of which something grows, something dark and terrible.

She throws her hands to her face, crying sounds unheard since
man came off all fours. Sounds primeval, bestial, forgotten by
the mind and locked deep in the animal voice box. Bitter animal
loneliness. Ashamed I laugh at her misery and walk away turning
around to look.

An old man, broken, bent, looking from eye's corner sees the
pretty boy girl crying. He moves slowly, cane coming near, kindly

old man, white-haired, twinkle in eye, gleaming gold in his mouth, "What's wrong child?"

Strange unanswering sounds from the beautiful lips and he comes closer.

"Beautiful child, don't carry on so. Here, here let me help you." Bold now, sits next to her, patting the beautiful head. Whispers to her, "Don't cry, I'll take care of you, come child."

Raises her from the bench and they disappear. Kindly old man, white-haired, twinkle in eye, gleaming gold in mouth leading a pretty boy girl.

WAS SATURDAY AT NANA'S, watching the world wake from my window. Early morning, people just beginning to stir. Mr. Charles came upstreet clucking Tomorrow, bell ringing. Suddenly sirens, flashing lights and police cars shattered the morning. Ten, twenty a hundred police filled the street. They'd trapped a killer in the building across the way. He'd killed and they came for him in blue numbers. Watched him firing while bullets chipped the brownstone all around him. He was charmed, none touched him. Blue police behind cars, windows and rooftops firing madly. Two broke from a hallway and sprinted for the building, running forward, stumbled still, dead. Another behind a car stopped firing. Two more died on the roof where the pigeon coop was. Their death bloodless and swift. Spotting me in the window across from him, he smiled and waved me down to safety. The noxious fumes, tear gas, burned my eyes and nose. They came at him from all sides, round after round sounding, someone shouted through a bullhorn, "Throw your gun down."

The smoke cleared and he flashed me a smile and high sign. Then threw down his guns, they fell five flights and clattered noisily on the ground. I saw it all from the window. They came in and stood talking. He had his arms above his head when they shot him and pushed him out the window. He fell gently, quiet, without violent movement, time froze, sickening sound of flesh smacking concrete. They let him lay there as an example to anyone who would try the way of the gun, running blood clotted in a puddle. People looked gawking and babbling about the crazy soul. Finally they came and got him, leaving only the bloodstain. Was sick all over myself, chills and fever, delirious. They put me to bed.

Looking out the window the next day saw the bloodstained walk, people stepping on it, only a few bothered to go around. The stain grew, turning bright red, covering the cars, people, buildings. Everything and body moved in it unconcerned. It climbed the walls and I screamed when it came through the window, warm and sticky.

Newspapers were full of the story of the berserk gunman. They told all, where and when he'd been born, what kind of person he was, the most insignificant details of his life became public record. Robles had overcome anonymity, for days people talked of nothing else. He's still alive, the warm smile and signs we'd exchanged. Something more had passed between us. I knew he wasn't crazy.

SHE LIVED ON THE THIRD FLOOR and we'd smiled and nodded at each other for years. It was cold and I was locked out. Stood in the hall window waiting for someone to come home and open the door. Saw her hanging out a window below, sensing eyes on her, she looked up and smiled.

"Hi George, locked out?"

"Cold isn't it? You locked out too?"

She showed me the latchkey on a string around her neck. All

the kids whose mothers worked wore them, but somebody was always home at our place.

"It's cold here. Why don't you come inside till someone comes?" Not waiting for an answer, she pulled me inside and left me standing in the living room. "Like some tea? Come in the kitchen, you can look out the front window."

Stood in the window watching the streets below.

"Look at that."

Turned to see what it was and she pressed up and kissed me. Taking my breath and rousing me.

"I'll get the tea, sit here."

"Why'd you do that?"

"Because I like you. Didn't you like it?"

Dared not raise my eyes and reveal my state. She asked me to put the dishes up, then grabbed me from behind and bit my ear. Held her away, not sure of what, and twisting, she was on me. Her wet snaking tongue fired me.

"Come on." In the bedroom she threw us down. Gaping, she put me in and began a rhythm, faster and faster. Had to pee. Lord. I had to pee. Held on till it hurt, felt her all slippery and wet inside. It began leaking and I jumped up and ran, pulling on clothes as I went, out and up the two flights of stairs. Burst through the door and ran to the bathroom, locking myself in. Stripped, watched the white substance spurting erratically from me, leaving me tingling and tired in my muscles.

Afraid of discovery, packed my underwear in a bag and carried it to the river. Stood in the mirror for hours brushing my teeth, trying to wash her germs and saliva out my mouth.

From that time evolved an idea of girls. The compatibility and sameness existing as children were gone. Unable to ride an elevator with a female unknowing the secret dark between her thighs. The young girls sitting gap-legged in class airing their hot bold pussies—wanted to come in all them and feel their small hard tits. Where once a meeting with a girl had been pleasure, were ever after anxious times. Immediately aware of their difference and my desire.

NANDY DRIFTS THROUGH MY MIND like a chimera, not announcing herself boldly, like herself, quiet. But everything centers round her, the focus of my thought and action. Nandy, for so long I'd turned thought from her, and she's the light in the dark. Memory of her is painful. In prison I dreamt constantly of her, longing is the most terrible pain in life. Having desire and powerless to satisfy even the slightest.

Don't know how I came to single her from the millions of people that crossed my sight. I was thirteen and child's innocence had gone, reality was stark and ugly. Began seeing her everywhere, school, playground, around the way. Out of politeness said hello. Hello turned to short conversations till seeing a friend and I'd abruptly end it and break away. Not wanting to be seen talking with a girl. Knowing they'd laugh. My people noticed.

"Georgie's got a girlfriend," my mother sang at the dinner table. She knew her name before I did.

I heard it first called by a girlfriend in the yard. Thought it a strange name, not knowing the feeling the two syllables would raise one day. To stop the banter, purposely avoided her, finding new routes to school and pretending occupation whenever we met. Passing her, her look of anticipation, greeting, then hurt and confusion as I went boisterously by with friends without a glance. Her brown eyes cut to the quick, shaming me and I ran back pulling her away from her friends.

"Hello Nandy."

"You don't have to talk to me if you don't want to, George Cain."
She said it so sad, turning away with a gesture of helplessness.

In those first days, we tried to give ourselves and capture each
other by relating entire histories. Recalling random memories,
anything that would help the other to better know and want
them. She told me of the South she was born in and returned to
every summer. Something all the black kids on the block did in
summer to gather strength for the cold northern winter.

"You going down South this summer?"

A place of freedom, barefoot and open. They'd come back sun-
browned, fat and talking niggerish to almost Christmas. I was the
only kid in the city during summer, all of my people were here.

Her influence on my life can't be told. She fired me with purpose. Would do all things for her. Saw each other only during
school. After school, she helped at home and I was playing ball.
When we met, we'd tell the other of all that had happened since
we'd been apart.

My life was no longer mine, but wholly bound in Nandy. Saturday, ice-skating in winter. She hurrying across the white ice, gay
garb, scarf flying. Sitting in the cold bleachers, warm and happy
with closeness. Her cheeks windburnt and red. Kneeling like a
gallant knight unlacing her boots with numb fingers. Her hand
rested on my shoulder, a queen's gesture, while I warmed her feet.
We'd walk home warming our hands in the other's, communicating by touch and pressure. How many times we'd lie together,
hugged up, afraid to let go, trying to overcome the flesh separating us and not knowing how. We cried, overcome by unnameable
fears and anxieties, the pain of our love.

I GO THROUGH ONE of the magazines. Been so long since I've
seen one. Cover picture, garishly lit street of the city. Stringed

lights, cars and neon stretching into blackness, recognize it, been there many times. Color so vivid, I blink rapidly to accustom myself. Have never seen the new electric colors of advertising before. First twenty pages or so filled with uninteresting advertisements, then a color spread of a little girl's body selling brassieres and filmy underclothes, run my fingers over the glossy sheet as if it'd turn to flesh. A reporting of news, editorials and black-and-white pictures and still I see the girl in filmy underwear before my eyes. A picture of two world leaders meeting, faces twisted into smiles and hands extended. How could anyone have confidence in their wasted faces straining to smile. An airplane crash, charred pieces and black crepe-covered dead. Gun-toting men and women, GUER-RILLA FIGHTERS. FLOOD STRIKES LOUISIANA, MILLIONS IN DAMAGE. On and on it went, the world wrecking itself. Feel so far away from it all. Like in the prison, nothing bothers or touches me, am safe and secure. No matter what happens out there, will not affect what goes on here or what happens to me. Nothing makes sense to me anymore. Have I been away that long? The text and logic of the statements in the mag are incomprehensible to me and I read like a foreigner, just looking at the pictures.

Turn the page and triggering memory of a former life, am overwhelmed, instantly transported to hot desert places.

Caravans in the Desert. Group of robe-bedecked Bedouins, camel-mounted, cast long shadows on the brown sand. The clearest blue sky and white sun shining down blind me. Hot brown sand sifting over sandaled feet and the white sun warm under a coarse wool robe. Unruly camels snorting, burdened under a load of dates and figs. They smell water. Give them their head and they step up. Jig, jog, sashaying from side to side, lulls me to sleep. Whistle splits the air, calling a halt and the camels squat to let us dismount. Unpack the beast letting it water and feed. Squatting, join my silent brothers in eating.

We come to the walled city, noise and gay colors relief from the oppressive desert. Veiled women and bazaars filled with spice smells and people. Crowds gathered about the storyteller, telling tales of former grandeur. Setting sun covers the scene in a rose light. Share the hookah, sucking on the pipe. Walk the dark maze of streets and alleys full of people and noise.

Zithers, drums and tambourines sound and passing through a curtain I join them. Bitter coffee and talk with a friend. Speaking the strange tongue with open mouth and clucking tongue against the teeth. Eat my lamb meal, heavily spiced and fragrant. Cloves and peppered sauce. Tired, head home and my silent woman waits for me. She's strong, dutiful and adores me, her man. It's getting cool and she fires the brazier, brings tea and the pipe. Lies by my side silently awaiting my pleasure.

The End.

Abruptly returned to the present by the rude ending and view the story again, trying to recapture it but it's gone and the magazine is again an incomprehensible sheet, making no sense.

Browse through another, pictures of tatter-clothed children, crowded stoops and dead people. Stare till recognition comes, it's the building I was born in. The same halls, swaying banisters, forty-watt bulbs and living statues frozen in time. The scene leaps from the page. Slam the book shut. The feeling of helplessness that came over me with Rosie fills me and I remember the trip to Lincoln Center. Know I won't make it.

"Wow. Just remembered something baby. The parole. Today's the day I'm supposed to show for the test."

"There's nothing we can do about it baby."

She throws it out of her mind, just like that, there's nothing we can do. Know he'll violate me, his sense of duty. Wonder how long it'll take to get word from D.C. Am truly fugitive now, from under their thumb, and again feel something lift from my heart and know I'm nearer freedom. They won't go through the expense of hunting me down, just wait for what they think inevitable, another bust and they'll stick it to me then. So sure I'll be scooped up by their dragnet of spies and police they'll not even bother to look for me. So long have I lived this fear that it's second nature like their death and taxes.

Nandy restores reality. "How we going to live baby? Can't have no life with the threat of prison hanging over us. Knowing you're a fugitive and liable to be busted any time. We can't live that way baby, ducking and dodging the Man, looking over our shoulder. Call that man baby, tell him something. Tell him you'll be there Monday, tell him anything."

Cannot believe just having freed myself from the Man, will now call him and beg to return and continue under the burden I've just dropped. But she's right. Am getting old. No longer have the energy of youth to sustain me. Until this moment, everything was done for the gratification of the moment, many moments and tomorrows were due me. Acted without knowing time or the importance of my acts, how they shaped my tomorrow. My life's history is a calamitous series of accidents that have brought me to this point. Where I who have never directed my life must now summon from somewhere the strength to do so.

I call Romo's office. He's not in but there's a message for me. The test has been put off till Monday, 9 A.M., without fail. We rejoice at news of my reprieve. Cannot believe my fortune and want to hurry this last twenty-four hours. Can begin life in earnest, cannot wait to try my hand at it. Hurt all over, but anticipating and planning my life drives pain out my mind. Cannot wait to feel as I felt a long time ago. To wake up in the morning feeling good cause I feel good. Not bound in the insulation of high that prevents my touching or being touched.

"Wow it's a good thing we called."

"Anyway I can use the supervision in the beginning. Not that I need it mind you baby, but it's another good reason for not fucken up."

"We'll make it baby and when you get off this thing we'll get up."

"Let's take a walk."

"You feel up to it?"

"Not far, just to Mount Morris."

We get down into the streets and the jungle roars, can feel it in my stomach. Am weak, but the streets give me energy and I feel better. Walk over to the park, passing so many of the dead on our way. Feel nothing for them and disgust for the profiteers. Police cruisers roll by and instead of cringing, throw head high. Am clean, free from my fear. There's nothing they can do or take from me. Before, intimidated by their presence and subject to arbitrary shakedown and arrest, my manner gave me away. But now they're servants in blue livery with gold buttons. In twenty-four hours have shed my past like snakeskin and walked away from it, emerging new and whole. We climb to the top of the park and view Harlem below us. Can see the boundaries on all sides, dark rivers and parks, natural boundaries cutting it off from the rest of the city. The climb has exhausted me and intensified the illness. Conga drums, deep and bass, sound all over, talking and answering. Feel them in my chest. Beyond the boundaries see the lights of the city like a red flame, all fire eating closer to the soft blackness, Harlem.

The drums get louder and more urgent, the flames closer. Looking out, see Harlem's in a valley. A pit, some great glowing hole. The drums pound in my head and we leave the park. Back in the room the monkey's still in his corner, twenty-four hours have come and gone without a fix and he's beginning to pale. In bed can still hear the drums. Try to sleep but my body will not function and the terrible craving begins. It has nothing to do with the pain or anything else. Total desire, need, every part of me screams for dope, want a fix so bad I'm going to step outside myself to get it. Fight and will with all my being, commanding my body to be still, knowing the slightest movement will send me running into the street.

My mind tires quickly, but the body besieged by cramps and denied its medicine allows no rest. How can it, missing a vital substance which I fed it daily for years to keep it functioning smoothly. Without it, nothing works, not even sleep, not with nerves jangling and jumping, quaking at center of self. Nandy, nothing she can do but watch helplessly as I fight. The demon leers from the corner, sure, unconcerned. He's been this way before and always emerged victorious, believes I have no strength or energy to fight him. Close my eyes, but pain clouds memory. Walk to the bathroom, loosing a strange colored liquid full of poison. Everything is falling apart, tearing down, trying to right itself. Struggling for normalcy without the poison, tragic magic. Felt so good once, thought it was God's medicine, cured all ills, unlike medicine, or anything else, it touched your soul, turning you strange, giving you eyes and awareness you'd not asked for. Turned black white and white black, oppressed you without an oppressor, jailed you without jail or jailer, locked you and your every fear inside you. The guile it worked on the mind, an unbelievable game it ran, making me believe that somehow I was together, hip. Hip is only a new way of dying. See the folly now and can't understand how I let myself fall this way. Junk attacks the body but is more than a physical ailment. It's the manifestation of a deeper ill. A decay in spirit. There is no God, but there's dope. A social, human, economic, physical, philosophical illness attacking every part of the man, brought on by every minute he's in this world. That's why I've retreated to this room and my mind into the past, for only in me, my history, can I find how to kill the monkey. That's where he came from, out of my head and past, full-grown and fingers locked on my throat.

THE DISORIENTATION AND CONFUSION BEGAN when I stopped going to church in Harlem. It was too long a ride. Instead going to the local white Presbyterian Church, it was more civilized and they recruited actively among the newly arrived project blacks. We'd been going about a year when Reverend White, the white minister, arranged for me to take the exam for Brey Academy, a very private school. Was four or five years after the '54 desegregation thing and niggers were fashionable. Everybody was wearing them to show how liberal they were. Studied all winter for the exam and that summer, was told I'd been accepted. The church and other organizations sponsored me. After a visit with the headmaster, my parents were convinced of the benefits of the school and determined that I go.

To the entire neighborhood I became the chosen one and was watched and prayed over. From then on, there would always be some white person behind me, going out of the way to help me, directing and controlling my destiny. I was a new toy, a novelty they couldn't believe, a nigger that could read and write, that was smart, maybe even brilliant. Something to be isolated and studied.

Started school that fall with leaves turning colors in the park across the street. Wore the school blazer proudly and loved the library with its endless volumes, furnished darkly, mahogany, musty and dim. Giant windows looking on the street and park. Matronly librarians moving on padded feet, dusting and arranging. The upper school and lower forms, steeped in tradition. Wanted to become a part of this.

Here was a strange world with different ways, accustomed to wealth, unused to hassling and scuffling. Life wasn't measured in days to payday or biweekly pay checks. To me, their ways were affected. To them, I was coarse and rude. They always appeared casually neat and I stiff and formal. When I imitated them by loosening a tie or button, was quickly called for being sloppy.

Mr. Twiceler at his raised desk recited the lesson in an English accent, impeccably attired, hounddog face, sagging jowls. Looking like he drank and never slept. High priest of the student intelligentsia. Leading them in culture. A fag draining come on the sly from his effeminate charges.

Dr. Queen looked down on me with the knowledge of histories long dead. Flaring red to the top of his bald head, shouted at me for laziness or poor posture.

Mr. Davis taught me German, pleased by my interest. He was a disgrace they said, filling the close winter room with sweet-smelling alcoholic breath, face lined by dissipation and bad living.

There was one other Negro at Brey Academy. Ralph Cotton was a pretty nigger, straight hair, light skin and Anglo features. A member of the Black Four Hundred, couldn't understand how his people didn't know mine and I was at Brey. All the black families that were into something knew of each other. They went to the same schools, belonged to the same fraternities, clubs and lodges. Went to Sag in summer, attended the same dances and social functions reported faithfully in *Jet, Ebony* and the *Amsterdam*. Where else were their sons and daughters going to find respectable friends and mates, equals among their own color, except in this parody of white society with debs, balls and tuxedoed escorts? And just as far removed and despising of the black mass as the white scene they slavishly aped.

Cotton would've preferred not to know me, but since we were the only two there, that was impossible. Our actions reflected on one another and the entire black race. To avoid embarrassment and sensing I was new to this world, he took me under his wing and made it his business to teach me their ways.

Cotton hated niggers like the Lord sin. They embarrassed and shamed him, reminding him of his color. We'd eat lunch in the park and he'd try to civilize me.

"Cain, you've got some ways about you that you're just going to have to change to get ahead in the world. The way you speak for instance. You should be more careful in your use and selection of words. Words such as *dig, cat, man,* they're inappropriate and reflect poorly on your background. You sound like a jazz bebopper, somebody off the streets, and anyway most of us don't use those words. You've got to remember George, other than their maids and servants, we're the only Negroes these people know and we must present a correct and favorable impression. You just can't act like a nigger, you've got to be better than them.

"Your accent, the way you talk, is due to nothing but laziness. Open your mouth when you speak and enunciate clearly. Slow down and take your time, think about what you're going to say."

It worked, in a few weeks everyone around the way commented on how properly I spoke. J.B. said I sounded like a faggot.

"Look George, why do you walk like that? You frighten people, stomping around like an ape. Relax, take it easy, what are you so tense about? Nobody's going to jump on you."

It took a greater effort to break the jitter walk that had protected me so long. Around the way, they said I'd gotten saditty. J.B. wanted to know when I'd started switching. But around the way and J.B. were no longer important or part of the life I wanted. Cotton and I succeeded as well as we could in overhauling my person, but there was nothing to be done about the hair, nose and lips, all of which I would've traded to complete the job.

After weeks of his tutelage, Cotton felt I was ready to debut and invited me to a dance his club was giving. The Jack and Jill Club of America, an arm of the NAACP, where young good niggers went to meet and be with other young good niggers.

Most of them lived in Queens and the dance was out there. Cotton met me at the subway in his father's car and we drove to his home to meet my date. Had wanted to bring Nandy, but Cotton needed a favor, someone to escort a family friend coming from New Orleans just for the deb ball. He was escorting the queen of the ball so couldn't do it. Had rented a tux that didn't fit too tough and the rain had knocked the creases out. His mother on seeing me insisted on pressing the wrinkles out while Sylvia, daughter of her best friend in college, was upstairs getting ready. Mr. Cotton was a little bald-headed man who jumped at her beck and call. While waiting for Sylvia, they questioned me about my family, background and plans. Who were my people, what schools did they attend, what did they do, what college did I plan going to? In the process, letting me know all these things about themselves. Since they couldn't list arrival on the *Mayflower* in their pedigree, they substituted learning and degrees. Education was the only thing they had to separate them in any way from the group and give them prestige. We've always esteemed learning, thinking it the key.

Mrs. Cotton left us men in the room and Mr. Cotton bragged on himself. He owned all the property and buildings for blocks around. But the niggers were destroying his property, thought they were down South or something. So used to outhouses, didn't know how to take care of a toilet, always dropping things into em and stopping em up. They'd been to Africa recently and he displayed souvenirs from the trip. All the while Ralph sat smugly knowing I was properly impressed. Had never seen or heard of legitimate niggers with what I thought then was money or living like they lived. Had thought the society columns in the black press were jive. Had never seen all those doctors and lawyers they'd be talking about.

Then Sylvia came down. Since Cotton wasn't taking her, didn't expect any prize and was struck dumb by this queen. She was physically the most perfect thing, couldn't believe she was going anywhere with me. Mrs. Cotton introduced us and then rehearsed me for our grand entrance. They'd had formal rehearsals for the march of the debs and escorts but neither of us had attended. Sylvia was familiar with the procedure and protocol down to the bow and curtsy but I had to stumble through it a couple of times till I got it together.

Was in the bathroom tidying up before we left and heard them talking outside. "Ralphie, where did you ever find him? Harlem? He's ugly as a nigger, big lips, wide nose, nappy hair and his hands sweat. He's not even one of us, he's a nigger."

"He goes to school with me. I didn't want to bring him. Mother made me. Told Mother what he was like, but she insisted."

"Now you children stop that talk, he might hear."

"Oh Auntie I'll be embarrassed to death with him. Nobody there knows him. They'll laugh at me in my new gown and his cheap rented tuxedo. You can tell, it doesn't even fit him. I'll just die being seen with him."

"I'm sure he's a nice boy and you'll have a good time. After all he's only an escort. You can have your picture taken with Ralph or any of your other friends. I'm sure they'll understand."

Stood studying my face in the mirror, trying to rearrange the big lips and wide nose. Felt ugly and knew I couldn't go to that dance cause I'd be the ugliest thing there. A hall full of beautiful people and one ugly nigger. Hated all people in that instant and forever more. Blacks, whites, rich and poor. Met rejection everywhere, there was no place for me and nobody like me.

Came out the bathroom and asked how to get to the subway. They understood, knew I'd heard and didn't try to stop me.

It was our private mystery. All the whites in school wondered why the only two blacks among them never spoke.

BASKETBALL WAS MY GAME and in October reported for tryouts. Balls slapping on hardwood, swishing through nets, cold gym, sneakers and body odors, a man holding a whistle.

"Say fellow what's your name?"

"Cain sir. George Cain sir."

"Go out and loosen up, let's see what you know."

They stood in little groups, watching and waiting their turn. Stood on the sidelines by myself.

"Hi, I'm Hannibal Ren the manager, was watching you, you're the best out there, a real natural."

In the weeks spent practicing we became friends. Two outcasts, he a Jew, banding against the others. We disliked them for their arrogance and indifference. His home on Riverside Drive was my first encounter with real money. A red and yellow uniformed doorman named Fritz let us in. "Master Hannibal and young friend."

Never saw such a place. Something from a magazine, paintings on the walls, carpets and beautiful furniture, nothing threadbare or shabby. His mother was hardly ever home, remember how he ran through the empty house calling for her. Then standing there ready to cry cause she wasn't in. Couldn't believe he had no brothers or sisters, everybody had brothers and sisters. Went by his house after school to study, was too noisy and crowded at mine, with Keith and the twins always around. He kept hinting, he wanted to come by my home and I kept putting him off with lame excuses.

My people were pleased at my progress and took great interest in everything. Wanted to know what I did and more important whom I associated with. I told them about Hannibal and the afternoons spent at his place. They were impressed by the address and never tired of my descriptions of the apartment.

"Son you've been to Hannibal's home and met his mother. You should invite him by here."

"What's the matter with you? Ashamed of us or something? Getting too good for us with your fancy friends. After all we've done for you. I'll pull you right out of that school. People filling your head with crazy ideas, turning you against your family and friends. We are hard working and honest, don't let anybody fool you into thinking they're better."

To restore peace I invited him for dinner. He accepted and the time was spent in anxious preparations.

"I'm glad you asked me George. Beginning to think you were like the others, because I'm a Jew . . ."

My mother cleaned and Pop wondered what he'd talk about and I hoped they wouldn't embarrass me. He arrived early and we sat in the living room. All I could see was the shabby furniture and cracked linoleum.

"Hannibal Ren, like you to meet my parents."

Stiff and awkward they met him formally like greeting royalty. Waiting for dinner, my father charmed us and filled the place with warmth, casting all my fears and shame away. They got on well together, had never seen this side of my father. His warmth and intelligence banished all formality and Hannibal never saw the naked walls or shabby furniture. The twins made Han read to them and tell about himself. My mother called dinner and we bowed to grace. Finished we sat around and they embarrassed me with their enthusiasm, asking him all kinds of personal things. Hated him then for causing me these feelings. Angry at everybody I tore him away.

"Dad, told Nandy I'd bring Hannibal by for a moment."

"Okay, but don't stay too long, it's getting late."

Was glad it was over, boiling inside with things I didn't understand. Her mother answered the door, shocked by my white friend and excused herself a moment while she ran to straighten the living room. Nandy came out and occupied us in the kitchen till her mother signaled. Don't remember what we talked about, only that they played a duet on the piano while I sat seething and wanting to run away. She kissed me and said something pleasant to him. Going down, he lagged behind looking back, saw him crying in the window. In that instant my heart softened. Ashamed of myself and loving everybody so intensely I cried too. Nandy waved from the window and we back, brushing tears from our eyes. Saw his face as the cab pulled away, tear-streaked and happy.

When the season began and my abilities became known, people sought me out, inviting me to their homes and parties. Was drifting slowly but surely from myself and began acquiring the traits which I'd thought most ugly in them. Their callousness, inability to feel, love. These things were weakness, I had to suppress and hide them to be like them. Till I was them. Young, urbane and sophisticated, white. Did not think of myself as black or white, but marginal man, existing somewhere in time and space on the edge of both. Rarely visited Nana any more, saw less of Nandy and around the way. Soon I knew no blacks and there was nowhere to see my oppression.

Everybody saw me changing and losing my way but said nothing. My people, Nandy. They felt it important that I know and be this way, giving me my head.

CHRISTMAS WAS COMING and the season in full tilt. We were undefeated and my name was in the papers. People who'd never noticed me began to. Was at a rally before the Fieldstone game that I accepted my fate. They were the traditional rivals in all sports.

Drums beating, stands full of lusty young voices chanting. "Beat Fieldstone! Beat Fieldstone!"

A pep rally, hate rally, drum booming. "Beat Fieldstone! Beat Fieldstone!"

Shouted by a thousand voices, sounding, resounding in the small gym. Contagious, warming to the core, infecting with violent passion. I shouted with them. Felt it flowing through us, one to another, we were joined in voice and desire. Was like being in church only easier to grasp than the elusive Holy Ghost. Noise ceased, leaving us limp and shaking with energy. I was proud of my school, Brey Prep, instilled with its spirit. They called me up to the stand. "That athlete who most typifies Brey Prep and the things it stands for, who's led our victorious team—George Cain."

Was there before them, seeing their many faces looking up at me. Loving them. Silence, sweating, subsiding emotion and I shouted, "Beat Fieldstone!"

Applause, drums booming. Shouting and jumping from the stand, I snatched a baton, raising them from their seats with my zeal, led the thousand in a snake dance. A thousand voices. "Beat Fieldstone, beat Fieldstone, beat Fieldstone."

A thousand pairs of feet shuffling and dancing crazy little steps till we all sat down, drained and exhausted. The day of the game, excitement, anxiety. Even the teachers were caught up in it and excused classes for the afternoon.

"How do you feel George?"

"Fine Mom."

"Then why aren't you eating?"

"Stop bothering him, he's got a big game tonight. Who you taking to the dance George?"

"Nobody."

"Nobody. What'd I tell you about that? Expect you to attend all social functions. Don't you realize they're the most important reason we're sending you to this school? So you can meet people and know how to conduct yourself. Boy you make me so mad sometimes, wasn't for this game'd make you stay home. An opportunity like this, any nice girl would love it. Nandy would've been perfect. Sometimes you act like you ain't got the sense you was born with. Let me explain to you why these things are so important. Do you realize business is conducted in a social atmosphere rather than in the office. In clubs, golf courses, over dinner, lunch, social gatherings, and this is why it's so important for you to attend these things. This is where things get done at. I don't care if you're not taking anyone, you stay and be seen at that dance, you understand."

Sat around after dinner till finally was time to go. As I left, my mother said, "The kids and I will be there to see you play tonight, your father has an important meeting and can't make it."

Didn't hit me till I was in the street. How'd they look among them people? Their Sunday outfits were out of time and place, not adequate for even a basketball game in my new world. People would gawk at them and know who they'd come to see. Their mothers and families would be there, but they were different. In that sad moment didn't want them to come, they'd shame me. Thought of not going to the game, conjuring reasons and excuses for their not showing. Hoping against hope they wouldn't come. Could see her cheering wildly and hugging me in front of all those people. Crazy thoughts ran in me and I knew shame.

Sat in the locker room, subdued, tying, retying sneakers, shaking with anticipation, thinking about my mother. Climbed the stairs to the gym. Hesitating, saw the gay colored bunting and scanned the huge crowd looking for them. Four thousand people roared as we came out and I tried to hear Mom's voice.

Shook hands and went up for the tip. We scored, they scored, supporters from both schools urging us on. The first half ended with us four in front. On the opening tap in the second half our center fell and his ankle blew up before our eyes. Unable to continue he left to applause and watched from the bench. One of our guards fouled out and they began closing. Didn't know for sure so engrossed in play but sensing it, the quiet from our side of the gym, we were falling behind. Tired, running, jumping, chest burning, gasped at air. Third quarter ended, down by eight. A silent minute rest. Could hear them shouting, "Beat Fieldstone!"

Playing center then. Tapping, return, dribble, shoot. Fake, shoot, shoot, run, shoot. Ball kept coming, was arm weary, playing by myself.

"Let's go George!"

Heard them shouting my name, urging me, wasn't tired, a second wind. Time out, their ball, in a huddle.

"Way to go Georgie. They're up by two, less than a minute. They'll freeze, we got to have the ball."

Buzzer sounded and play resumed. Came down slowly, freezing the pill. Steal, break and lay it up. Their ball, bad pass, break, jam with both hands and come down court swapping fives. Noise is deafening, drums and pounding on bleachers. They come down, pass and score. Tie game, dribble down court, crowd counting the seconds trying to hurry the shot.

"Five, four, three . . ."

Nobody open, fired off balance.

"Two, one."

Shot hung in the air, but I knew it was good when it left my hand. There was stillness, then all hell broke. Heard Mom's voice in the roar and looked over the crowd to find them. Saw her waving across the distance, impossible to get to. Hannibal was holding one of the twins up to see and Keith had climbed to the top bleacher shouting his head off. Made it to the locker room. Sat there, suddenly fatigued, hearing the congratulations, handshakes and back pats, not wanting to ever move. Had seen Mom in Sunday, strange and out of place, calling her baby. Not wanting to ever leave there, remain forever in the warmth of victory. No one knew the score except we'd won by two. Scorekeeper came down with the book.

"Seventy-six, seventy-four. George you set a record, forty-six points. Way to go, they're waiting for you upstairs."

Sat looking at the green lockers, hearing the shower drip and Hannibal came in. "Your mother's waiting for you downstairs. Beautiful game man, beautiful."

Dressed slowly, hoping they'd leave by the time I got there. She hugged me, the twins irritable and tired after their bedtime whined for me to pick them up and Keith kept dunking shots in the wastebasket. Was glad everybody was upstairs. She pressed a few dollars on me. "Go on up now and have a good time."

Kissed her and the twins, threw Keith a pass behind my back. Watched them walk down the block and vanish into dark. Could see the projects down there all lit up, seemed a long way from here. Ran downstreet shamed and crying and kissed her again, uncaring who saw. Unused to the affection but pleased, she smiled love on me. Walked back to school blinded with tears, full with love.

Hannibal met me at the door, "Something wrong George? You look funny. They're waiting for you upstairs."

The gym was loud, band playing in jump time, rock-and-roll music, a spotlight roamed the dark, bodies huddled close moved zombie-like, in time, out of time. The light picked me out and everyone turned. Band played a fanfare and four thousand eyes held my image. Bathed in light, I knew finally what it was all about. Fuck the school, the team, it was me they looked at, the adored one.

"Here he is, the hero of tonight's game. Scored forty-six points, the greatest single performance in the school's history. Come on up George, let the people see you."

They opened a path, anticipating me like some huge ship cutting through ice and fell back to let me pass. Entering the gates of the city, riding an ass, they spread palms before me, shouting hallelujah. Stood above them, looking down, wanting to say something great, memorable, and uttered a feeble thanks. Coming off the stand, was surrounded. Introductions, invitations, congratulations, all those who'd seen and been indifferent to me so many times, shaking my hand and wanting to know me. People I didn't know led me around and introduced me to their friends. Enhancing themselves by linking themselves to me, sharing my triumph, basking in reflected light, illuminating their spheres with my radiance. Couldn't have it. Had to get out in the air, away from these thieves of triumph. Where was Hannibal? I fled.

Walking in the park to get it together, warm with victory, an unfamiliar voice called. Bennet Shapiro, president of the junior class, came walking up smoking a pipe. "Hi man, too much in there? Like a madhouse, had to come out and get some air. What you doing tonight? Why don't you come with me, going to make a few parties. Be boss, wine, women . . ."

He laughed gaily, uncontrollably, bordering insanity. His upturned face, strong and Judaic, with a Jew's pain and passion. I felt he was somehow different from the rest. He was a white nigger, more familiar with the argot and life-style than most niggers I knew. My self-discovery began with his interest and discovery of me. Befriending me cause I was black and therefore, he thought, hip and into something. Hung with him for his money and good times, acted the role to keep him happy and learned to dig it.

"Why not, I put myself in your hands tonight."

"Good, here, smoke my pipe." Took it, sucking gently, unused to smoking. Strong acrid smoke burnt my chest, filled head and lungs. Choked, it burst from eyes, ears and nose.

"If you're going to waste it, give it back. Look, like this, hold it down, otherwise you're just wasting it."

Tried again, filling, fogging my brain, lifting me high in the air. Going mad and thought I was God. My mad laughter rattled through the woods. Awareness, no God, is God, I was God, silence. State of consciousness somewhere between conscious and subconscious usurped the mind, not subconscious for I was aware of it, not conscious for I had no control of it, strange level of consciousness that uttered obscenities and heresies.

"Stop."

But on it went. Set up interference, by rambling in my conscious mind, alleviating the pressure and finally it ceased. Was madness, was on the brink of insanity. Tempted to go beyond and deny all responsibility. Stopped by something I didn't know but just a bit more promised success and I sucked hard. A fine crystal awaiting a pure sweet note to shatter me into a million pieces, but it passed, resolving into euphoria.

"Say what is this?"

"Hashish, hash, fun toying with insanity isn't it?"

He'd been there too.

We returned to get our coats. The dance was breaking up and couples stood around planning their parties.

"Hey Georgie, see you at the party."

Nodded amiably, no longer could they take anything from me, triumph I'd secured deep inside me.

"Come on Cain, my car's around the corner."

A foreign-made sports convertible. Though cold, we put the top down, warm in a drug stupor. Speeding through Central Park, empty at the late hour, wind snatching at hair and face.

Racing through it, laughter leaving us bubbling, light. Red lights passed in rapid succession. How fast, 100, 110, 120 and blackness flying by. Heard them coming, sirens wailing, telling us to stop.

"Let's run them." Made the turn at 59th Street. There were two of them distant fading into night.

"Let's stop and wait for them to catch up."

They came hurtling round the corner, braking, spotting our lights, pulled up on the grass. "Sonofabitch, what the hell you doing, trying to kill somebody?"

Came near, metal shining, badges, guns, visored helmets, storm-trooper stride, silly looking. Unable to contain our laughter.

"Young punks, let me see your license and registration. Speeding, passing a red light."

"They ain't got no alcohol in the car. Here, hope you two smart bastards kill yourselves."

Laughing, exited on Central Park South going east.

First party was on Sutton Place overlooking the East River. A dark apartment, music, reefer passing round. Greeted by an unseen host and introduced to a hundred faceless people. Separating sexes by sound and touch. They couldn't see me. Light, wanted light so they could see me. Triumph stolen into darkness. Held someone close, female breasts stabbing, pelvis extended, dry fuck, whisper in ear, moist tongue, frantic words, hot breath, her shuddering, shaking, moaning, coming in her clothes, sweet scent rising to my nose. Leave her to find another, groping, feeling my partner race in me for a moment, discharge and go find another. A merry-go-round, exhausting, wasting myself in hurried love affairs abridged to a dry fuck, lasting long as a three-minute record.

We left the party and returned to Central Park South, smoking hash and caught up in senseless giggling jags. Silly, unable to stop. Entering the building, rode an elevator to the top of the world. Heard a band playing soulless music for dead people. A penthouse, occupying the entire floor. Full of beautiful people in beautiful clothes.

"George Cain, you made it, everybody look who's here."

Eyes of all those beautiful people fell on me, adoring, swarming about to touch, speak with me. Was I real, it real? Now seeming fantasy, but then too it was fantasy. Beautiful and inviting, waiting for me to arrive and take my place in it. Joan came to me from out of their many faces, her beauty demanded acknowledgment.

"So you're Georgie Cain, have heard lots about you from my brother, saw you play tonight, you were beautiful."

Stood agape while she rambled on, her brother was someone or other I went to school with. Laughter, her beautiful laugh, how easy it had been, sophisticated children playing adults.

"Have a drink." A drink I didn't need, thinking it would sicken me, but took it obediently.

"Have you ever seen the city from this high up? Come see."

How high up were we? How high is high? Saw the city for the first time, not looking up to it, a part of it, one of the silhouettes in a window I'd seen so many times from the ground below.

Central Park stretched below, patched and illumined green by streetlamps. The duck pond mirrored the night moon, water, light-streaked reservoir further up, the castle, the black wall bordering 110th Street. Had I seen all those things in the dark or put them there from memory? Didn't care. High above pedestrian noises, traffic, time had stopped. Unhearing noise at my back, her breathing, unaware of all presence except myself and the city below. Nodded dumbly to her queries trying to prolong the moment. Then it happened, could see that part of the city where I came from, opening, black, filthy smelling. A cavernous mouth, dark mystery, its red garish lights, a tongue stretched through darkness coming near. Paralyzed with fear stood awaiting it. From the monster throat, beautiful music, bewitching. Sirens singing and calling to me. From deeper down in its belly came familiar voices, my mother, father, Nana, Aunt, Nandy, calling me.

It was gone, receding into night.

"It's pretty isn't it?"

Stammered something and turned to hide my face.

"Would you take me home?"

"I don't have a car."

"Mine is downstairs."

"Don't know how to drive."

"I don't make it a habit to ask people to take me home. This is the first time."

"No, you don't understand, I want to, but really I've never driven a car."

"Well come on I'll show you."

Looked for Bennet to tell him not to wait and left with her. Felt uncomfortable being piloted through dark streets by the competent young girl, wondering how the evening would end, goodnight kiss, handshake, plain good night. Aware of our close-ness, narcotic-heightened sensibility, heat stifling me in the close vehicle.

"Come up for a while."

A quiet building like some inner sanctum, pharaoh's crypt, unlike the noise-filled places in which I'd lived. Walked lightly, tipping.

"Why are you walking so, there's nobody here, my parents are away for a while, it's the maid's night out. Here, give me your coat."

Stood in the living room afraid to sit, afraid to break some-thing with my huge frame. Furniture so fine, thought it orna-mental rather than functional. She found me standing when she returned. "Sit down and I'll make something to drink."

Watched her move through the place. She was bred to this life, while I had only recently arrived. She shuffled through a pile of records choosing one, then sat me down. Silent, not knowing what to say to each other. Sipping drinks, our silence threatening eternity.

"Why are you so quiet George? Other fellows I know chatter away, telling about their petty triumphs and conceits. You seem reserved, older. This your first year at Brey? Where did you go before? Public school, what was it like?"

In the telling of it all our adult sophistication vanished, and reduced to the children we were, we abandoned ourselves to laughter and silliness. Alcohol made us giddy. Holding hands, looked into each other's faces, kissing, clinching, baiting passion, enjoying restraint.

It might have come through a door or open window, so suddenly was it upon me. Felt it moving urgently through me, filling me with lust. Heat, stifling, tore at each other, saying the crazy words, wanting and not wanting her in the same instant. Her feeble protest only adding to the frenzy. Took her clothes off her and her shut legs came apart. I entered. Tearing and ripping through virgin membrane, her screaming in my ears, biting and snorting. Crying, then wanting it, begging me. Coming, coming then gone. Resting my head on her stomach, soft hair, flesh of underbelly, coarse pubic hair. Saw the virgin's blood dripping and drying between her legs. Thanking me. Felt it rise in me so many times that long night. A strange lovemaking, all pain, biting and claws, sleep came easily.

Waking and still high, looked on her ashamed of what had been done, of my nudity. Washing, saw myself and felt violated, vilified. Unworthy of Nandy. The things we'd said and done. Felt filthy, covered with slime, wanting to tear my skin and bleed it from me. Had to get away from her, into the air, away from her. Grabbed up clothes, running. She hung on me as I tried to escape. Asking a woman's insanities. Did I love her? Answering, yes, yes, yes to anything, just wanting to get away. Frightened I ran, walked, ran again till I was exhausted. Stopped, looking about. Lost—where was I? Recognition came slowly, it was Harlem. Standing across from the church I hadn't entered since Granny had died in the fire. Went in. At the altar, there was a resurrection in me of things thought long dead and forgotten, the warm yellow-colored love. Fell on my knees, raving forgotten prayers to statued Christs. Seeking absolution, heard myself, sounding odd, like young Georgie. Walked into black streets, crowded with people, feeling their number and movement in my gut.

While waiting for the subway, resolved never to see her again. Bought a *News* and turned to sports section, BREY PREP NIPS FIELDSTONE, GEORGE CAIN STARS, SETS SCORING RECORD. Turning to the back page, stared at a picture of a neat smiling Negro boy. Unrecognizing myself till I read the caption and saw my name. Smiling, a posed picture taken in dress clothes for the yearbook at the beginning of the term. It was me. Train came, crowded. Folded the paper and sat looking round, my image at every turn, everyone reading the same paper. How many papers did they make? A hundred thousand, a million, how many saw the counterfeit image? Then wondering what's wrong with them, couldn't they see it was me, Georgie Cain, and I assumed the picture's expression. Maybe I wasn't real, maybe they weren't real, but I was real, look there, my picture. But they were blind to me. Jumping from the seat, pulled the paper out and screamed at them, "Look it's me you're looking at! I'm real, can't you see me?"

They looked and turned away when our eyes met. Couldn't they see or hear me? Wanted to snatch their papers, all million of them and cut the picture out. As I exited, heard a little boy talking, "Mom that man said that was him in the picture."

"No son, just someone that looks like him."

The train left the station, stood watching it leave, pulled the paper out and burned it.

Woke early the next day, everyone was in church, they no longer made me go. The events of the night before plagued me and I hurried out to find Nandy. She'd come from church dressed in Sunday. Took her arm, happy to be close, guilt and care gone at the sight of her. She was quiet and strained. Sitting doe, the sad eyes.

"What's wrong baby?"

She didn't answer right away, gathering strength to utter the thought. "I've got to stop seeing you."

She spoke slowly, tear-choked. Waited for the words to affect me. There was nothing at first. So alien the thought. Me without her, not seeing her or loving her had never crossed my mind. Ice was my heart and I wanted to scream and stop hurting.

"Who doesn't want you to? Tell me. Who?" Wanting names, objects for the hate in me. "Your mother?"

She nodded. Felt myself losing control, seeing myself without her. Suspected her mother's disapproval ever since the private school. Nandy was the oldest child and she and her mother were close, in nothing had Nandy ever disobeyed her. My hate became anger—wanted her to hurt like I was hurting, wanted her to struggle it out painfully—and returned it to her untouched, undiminished. "What do you want to do?"

Watched her turning it in her mind. Trembling lips and sniffles the only sign of struggle. A shudder passed through her and I knew she'd decided. Wanted to erase the conversation from mind, begin again and find some compromise that allowed me to see her. Wanted to tell her, let's take some time to think about it, anything, a few days guised in indecision, but don't leave.

"Whatever you want me to."

Her feeling was mature and sensitive, she'd come from under

the parental yoke to submit and mingle her life with mine. The words we spoke were as binding as any contract, obligating and making me responsible for her. We made love that day and my thing for her was all consuming, giving me new ambition and desire. She was reason for my existence. A week later her mother had her in South Carolina.

Alone, without her, sank into myself and let go. There was no longer any reason for anything since I'd done everything for her, just didn't care.

George Cain, George Cain. Everyone knew and called my name. Joan called the house dozens of times, Bennet had given her my number. I was not in and refused to answer till one day my father got tired of it.

"Look, this girl calls you every day, at least have the decency to call her and say you don't want to be bothered. Son you've got two years of school left, then college. Your mother and I have worked hard to make you ready to put you where you're at. About Nandy, she's a good girl and everything, but what if something were to happen, I know she's a nice girl but accidents . . . Not saying she's a chippy or out to snag you. But you'd be a prize with all your possibilities and these things do happen and your mother and I didn't sacrifice for that. You can have that any time, there are a million girls out there who'd love to go out with you. You're young yet, knock yourself out, there'll be plenty of time for love."

Remained silent through the tirade, a coward, didn't deserve Nandy. Stayed in my room for days sulking, avoiding friends and family. She wrote me, she understood all. Told of my father's speech, she agreed that it was best.

So many things worked me. My life was spent gratifying other people, all my efforts were for them.

Was spending a week with Bennet, his parents were in Europe

somewhere and I was keeping him company. So casual and unconcerned about their people, he and all the kids were. Began to think my concern was the result of low breeding. Everyone else seemed obliged only to themselves, while I was striving for Brey Prep that had given me a scholarship, my mother, father, brothers, people, for the sacrifices and faith they'd placed in me. Everyone but me had a piece of George Cain. Was no longer me, but a composite of all their needs and desires.

"Did you dig your picture in the paper man? You're a celebrity man, big time. You split from the party with Joan, she's something else, her people got money. Gave her your number, hope you don't mind. She says you ain't never in. Why don't you call her now? I've got a chick coming over later and we can party."

"Hello Joan? Cain."

"Oh yes, the celebrity, how are you today? I'm sorry George, don't want to be a bitch with you. I love you, how are you. Been calling you all week and they keep saying you're not in, so happy to hear you. What are you doing now? Why don't you come over. See you in an hour." The phone clicked.

"What'd she say?"

"Invited me over."

"Dig, why don't you make it and I'll catch you later. Got some business to take care of."

He left me under a street lamp and I headed to her full of desire and expecting fulfillment.

THE PHONE RANG AT DINNER ONE NIGHT, my mother answered and called my father from the table. They told me to watch the kids and left. Keith sensing something cried himself to sleep. They returned late with Auntie Flo, haggard from their vigil. The building had burned again and Nana was in the hospital.

Couldn't believe, wouldn't, my birthplace was gone. That place, a scene for much of my life gone. An image was before me, the dark halls, forty-watt bulbs, dumbwaiter and people. The picture was before my eyes, in my head and no longer real. Began crying and they thought for Nana, but it was for the past gone in smoke that I cried. It was late. The family had regained its composure. Nana was going to be all right and we were all going to live together again, when the boy came with the telegram of death. My father called me into his room.

"George, Nana is dead."

Shut out the words, not believing.

"Yes son, she passed this evening."

I froze, couldn't cry, scream or anything. Tried to think of death, till that moment never having known it. Believing child-ishly the world was dependent on consciousness. But Nana had gone and the world was still here. What was this death, a willful rejection of life. She'd grown weary, been here long enough. Only the women had time for grief. Next day my father and I were at the ruins for salvage and a list of destroyed articles for the insur-ance people.

The building was a charred shell but such a moneymaker they'd rebuild it, soaked and smelling burnt. Closets were open and the contents strewn all over. Walls and doors ripped and gashed by axes, drawers scattered, everything of value gone. Pop found the family photo album soaked and laid it in the window to dry. I found the huge foil ball he'd collected when a child. Heard someone moving in the hall. There were three of them. The hall statues had come to life. Looked into their six red eyes and saw the sacks on their backs and remembered Nana's warnings. Rogues and scavengers she'd called them.

"What do you want?"

"Same thing you do sonny."

Knew they were combing the ruins for valuables.

"You're too late, everything's gone."

"What's that you got in your hand?"

"None of your business."

"Fuck you."

He came close to take it from me, his two partners smiled wetly, licking lips. Felt myself fill with murderous rage at God and man. The ball busted his head open, blood jumped everywhere. He pinned my arms and smothered under his liquor breath, I bit into his face and spat out blood. He screamed and we tumbled down a flight of stairs knocking against the wall and banister. Pounded his head with the ball, he kicked and rolled like a snake. They pulled me off and rescued him, dragging him into a burnt out apartment for first aid. Screamed and shouted like crazy, my father came, saw the blood, them disappearing and me raving mad. Frightened by my eyes and expression took me to a doctor. Lay in bed long weeks sedated and recovering. Never saw Nana in bier or put in the ground.

All was over when I returned to the world, spent and exhausted. Nana was gone and there was no reason to ever come back here, cut off from the source. Grew to loathe and fear Harlem, like some pit or horror escaped, into which I never wanted to set foot again.

WHAT DROVE ME TO HARLEM two years later? Riding a bus through it, but never getting off, was a favorite thing that summer. Watched the people through the glass, like observing an ant colony, felt their heat pressing on the bus, their noise rolling in waves over my ears. Traveled there high on wine and hash. Would see and recognize landmarks from childhood whose secret places I knew. In one of my stupors the song of their voices called me and I got off. Walked among them, feeling their press, presence, their blood flowing in me, me in them, felt welcome, the prodigal returned after a long absence. Walked the endless pavements gathering strength.

Was sixteen, six-three and mustached, looking like a man. Was on one of these walks that I met Jose, hadn't seen each other since the Y. He was sixteen too, but the eyes and face were old, jaded. The clothes he wore were not of his age, belonging to an older generation. Pointy shoes, long-collar shirt, pleated baggy pants, expensive and beyond the price and taste of a child. Baggy pants bop, hustler.

"Come on with me Georgie, someplace we can talk."

Walked with him through the crowded streets. He knew everybody, waving and rapping with the young foxes and old folks. Kids called his name and he passed out nickels, smiling, stopping to say a word here or there. Went to a bar, the first I'd been in, and he ordered drinks. The other patrons hailed him, he waved back. Looking around, saw they were older but similarly dressed, like a uniform of some trade or profession I didn't know.

"Hey Jose who's that with you?"

"Remember the ballplayer was showing you cats in the paper all winter. The one I told you I grew up with. Cain, this is him."

"How you been Jose?"

With a gesture, indicated his clothes and displayed rings on his fingers.

"Right after we quit the Y, get into some trouble, ran away from it and been here ever since. Running digits, selling a little dope, got an old lady. Hustling, that's all, just hustling. Been keeping track of you in the paper, always knew you'd make it."

"Ever see Robert or Bushy?"

"Yeah, they're all fucked up."

"Where are they? Like to see them."

We left and he led me to a condemned building. Down a dark cellar and through a door guided by smells of alcohol and stink of bodies. A bunch of people huddled on a raggedy mattress on the ground. He roused two of them and signaled to follow and we escaped into the air.

"Bushy? Robert? You remember Georgie?" He spoke to them as if recalling them from far away. Both shook from their need and stared hard at me, but nothing showed in the vacant eyes. He stopped at the wine shop, bought a bottle of Gypsy Rose and gave it to them. They stood around shuffling and grateful like pets, animals. Tragic figures, comrades of youth, already dead. Their lifeless eyes avoided me, impatient to be gone about their self-destruction. We got up and left them to their killing.

That summer, beginning and ending in Harlem, place of birth. A time recalled in brightness, full of discovery. Made daily excursions to the sector, reacquainting myself with its ways and people. Saw Robert and Bushy, always haggard and gaunt, sinking before my eyes. Wanted to talk with them, find out, but they never spoke. Jose and I got tight, we'd meet and hang out in the bar. Sometimes I'd sit up and rap with Stacy, an oldtimer. He'd been a player, one of the successful few, owned the bar and other real estate. Their dress, baggy pants bop, was the style all the young niggers aspired to. Peculiar to them was a culture, language and code. From Stacy I learned the strange words and heard the glorified romances of its heroes and heroines. Boxcar Shorty, Thousand Dollar Red, hardhearted men, run a whore till her feet sharp as deer hooves. Marguerita, Du Fontaine, whores who took a trick for all he had and brought it home to daddy, and the police who extorted, busted and slept with them. Was awed by these people. Fooled by the cheap glamour not knowing it was all show. A game of survival.

Came in off the hot streets and Stacy called me over.

"Hey slim. Man, you make an ass out of Sporting Life, nothing to do but sit around and look slick. Been playing any ball lately? How you going to be in shape when the season starts? You going to college? College costs a lot of scratch, you got to get a scholarship man. Know your people ain't got that kind of money. But that shouldn't be no big thing good as you play, unless you fuck up, keep hanging out here. Look around you man. You don't see no doctors, lawyers, teachers, ballplayers, college grads. Look at them good, all dressed in nice expensive clothes. Should all be familiar to you long as you been coming here. Ain't none of em got more'n two outfits to wear. One on their backs and one in the cleaner, everything else in the shop. They got cardboard in their shoes and wash their drawers every other night in the facebowl in their rooms. Clothes look good on thin men, but these cats ain't models, they that way cause they hungry. You know what they sit around here waiting for all day and night? The big sting that'll never come. That's what they're laying for. Sitting around talking about that big money, their old ladies out there turning nickel tricks. You done heard me talk about this game, but how strong a motherfucker got to be to take money from a bitch? Dig em sometime when they high, one of them unconscious moments and they look like bitches. They got to glorify this game cause everybody knows where it's at. It ain't shit.

"You got eyes for this thing, hustling, but it ain't nothing but degradation. You got it made Georgie, don't fuck with this thing. Why do I tell you this? You were born here so was I, Jose and all the rest and we'll never get out of here, but you're different man, you're out there. Why you came back I'll never know, but you got to make it. Not just for yourself, but for your family, friends, all of us here that ain't never going to make it. How many generations come and gone, how much sacrifice to make one like you? Your life ain't your own boy. Don't seem right do it? You and your kind are the lambs of the sacrifice, when enough of you get out of this place, we'll all get out. The time wasn't right for your father, or me but now's the time and you can't hesitate. You got to be clean, and pure so you'll be strong for what's out there. Why else would your people have had you, only the hope of you redeeming them, us, from this. For us to bring children into the world without hope or future is sin. This is the only reason for you being man, but you got to be strong, too many are weak and come back, need this, like Jose. There are enough of us here George. We can't do no better, go away, stay away."

WAS COLD OUT and a strange moon hung in the sky. Rain fell in gray windblown sheets. Wet to the bone and cold. Saw the Gunsmoke ahead, good place to be that night, high and drunk. Noise, rocking and festive spilled into the streets, hot breath clouded the windows telling of the good time inside. Was Saturday night. Came in cold, wet, waved to Stacy tending bar. Jose hadn't showed yet so sat up in the corner waiting. He came in blowing cold out and waving to everybody. He'd cracked on me before to get high with him on stuff but I'd always nixed it. Afraid of its power. Maybe it was the funny moon that night, have never seen another like it since, but I was swayed, got down with him.

Went out the back way, through the yards. Howling dogs and cats sent startled beady-eyed rats scurrying over our feet. Like the streets, yards full of garbage and stink, tripping on every snatching thing. Till we came to the door he pushed in. Led up the stairs, pulling a package out of the old unused dumbwaiter shaft and ducked into a room. Checked the hall and locked the door and pushed a chair against it. Looked out the window and pulled the shade.

"Man, you sure you still wanna do this thing? I'm sorry I asked you now."

"Yeah man, I done come all the way up here now."

"You know what you doing now George? Don't want you going round telling people no shit. I gave you your first shot of dope, like I tied you up, twisted your arm or something."

We'd come to this point before and I'd always back out at the last minute. Had watched him hit himself many times and wondered what he was feeling.

"Dig man, I know what I'm doing, get on with it."

He draws up and the needle strikes my arm like a live thing to suck my blood. He squeezes the bulb shooting heroin on a dizzying flight. Moving in the vein a rush of air bubbles pass under the armpit. For an instant all is still and I see clearly, through God's eyes. Then it's upon me, bursting from every pore. Full with it, swoon at the impact. Suffocating, heart and lungs in a tightening vise, gasping, body demanding blood and air. Squeezing again the blood full dropper. Running red hemo, raging in me like a Niagara fed river, red, taxing flexible carriers, storm fed, wild running thing, threatening dikes and levees. My knees buckle and dizziness rocks me. Then calm, terribly sudden and infinite, aware only of self, shut off from objects and distractions. Nausea again. The torrent has not ceased, only run deeper till it found an outlet, spewing from my mouth and splashing into the tub with all its former vigor till there's nothing in me. It comes over me warm and substantial. Prying open a lid, watch Jose clean the equipment. Sit thinking nothing, just glad to be, nodding and scratching. Scratching my legs and crotch like a louse-filled beggar. Scratching seems the most gratifying thing in the world.

From there my fall from grace was swift. Junk, it was what I'd been born for, waiting for all my life. There are no accidental junkies, nobody can tie you up and string you out. You have to work hard to get hooked, takes too much time and effort to be an accident. You have to like and want it long before you need and crave it. It is not till many fixes pass that your desire is need. You're given many warnings along the road to hell. Turn back, danger ahead they say but you plunge recklessly on cause you're different, stronger than the others already hooked. You alone have something all the others don't that'll keep you from being a slave. Laugh, cause junk don't give a fuck bout nothing or none of ya'll, don't discriminate a bit, try it and can't nothing save you from the conclusion, addiction.

HAVE GONE FAR AS I CAN, exhausted the file on myself. The rest occurred during my wanderings in the desert when I raged out of my mind and cannot be sure of what did and didn't happen. There were no landmarks or guideposts. Only the addiction pushing me after the next fix. All those dead wasted years from which I recall nothing but the pain. The sun is up and I watch one-two-five, 125th below me. It's near noon, Nandy's washing, getting ready to go eat. Look at myself in the mirror to see any change in my face, the skin and eyes—pupils are larger than ever. Moving around, feel and hear my bones scraping against one another, thirsty, the body has passed out all liquids to remove the poison. My skin is dry and grainy, funny to touch. Stench of junk clinging to it. Afraid to bathe and open my pores, would make me more vulnerable to sickness. Junk is a boss medicine and preservative. During its tenure remarkably free from the common illnesses that plague man, but the moment it is gone, everything comes down on you, cold, toothaches, everything.

"How you feel baby?"

"Hurt all over. Everything hurts."

"Coming down with me to eat?"

Sit up in the restaurant while she eats, drinking coffee and glasses of water. See myself in the mirror, outwardly calm and normal, nobody would suspect the intense pain of my detoxification. Finished we walk the streets, and everywhere I see the demon, on every corner dealers with pockets full of poison. We stop at a stand selling all sorts of African jewelry and I spot this necklace with a monkey's head. Just like the monkey that haunts me. I buy it and throw it on. He hangs round my neck and the hunger shall always be a threat. The streets make me feel better, they're part of my addiction, not the junk alone. Spy a clock, one-thirty, seventy-two hours, three days have passed, have beaten the monkey. Look up and everything looks different somehow. Like I'm seeing the world for the first time in a long time. I hold Nandy tight, handcuffed so I don't break away.